A solitary man stands on a lonely beach, gazing out at a shipwreck which he has miraculously survived. He must now face an untamed island and conquer nature to exist. The man is called Robinson. Thus the scene is set for the familiar Robinson Crusoe theme—but this is not just another retelling.

The author, Michel Tournier, soon departs from the traditional story and gives it a fresh and totally relevant life. It is the old tale, but told with new action and insights, carrying Robinson through both physical and psychological experiences on Speranza Island. A most unexpected twist occurs in the master/slave relationship of Robinson and the Indian, Friday, when their roles are curiously reversed.

With skill, Michel Tournier weaves a clever and fascinating story for readers, young and old.

FRIDAY AND ROBINSON

Life on Speranza Island

by

Michel Tournier

Translated by Ralph Manheim

drawings by David Stone Martin

ALFRED A. KNOPF NEW YORK

Library of Congress Cataloging in Publication Data
Tournier, Michel.   Friday and Robinson: life on Speranza Island.
SUMMARY: A new approach to the Robinson Crusoe story which explores
Robinson's psychological as well as physical experiences and introduces
a new twist—Friday eventually becomes master of Robinson.
Translation of Vendredi; ou, la vie sauvage, a version for children of
the author's Vendredi; ou, Les limbes du Pacifique.
[1. Survival—Fiction.] I. Tournier, Michel. Vendredi; ou, Les limbes du Pacifique.
II. Martin, David Stone, illus. III. Title.
PZ.T6475Ve Fic 78-39598 ISBN 0-394-82414-8 ISBN 0-394-92414-2 (LIB. ED.)

FRIDAY AND ROBINSON

PROLOGUE

Late in the afternoon of September 29, 1759, some four hundred miles off the coast of Chile and not far from Juan Fernandez Islands, the sky suddenly darkened. The crew of the *Virginia* gathered on deck to watch the lightning that played about the sky. It was a sign that a bad storm was coming. Luckily the *Virginia*, on which Robinson was a passenger, was equal to the worst of storms. She was a Dutch galliot, short-masted and broad of beam, which made her heavy and rather slow but remarkably stable in bad weather. So that night when a violent wind arose and one of the sails burst like a balloon, Captain Van Deyssel ordered his men to lower the other sails and wait below for the storm to pass. The ship could handle anything but reefs and sand banks, none of which were charted in the region, and there was every reason to believe that the *Virginia* could safely run before the storm for hundreds of miles.

The captain and Robinson settled down to a quiet game of cards while the storm raged outside. At that time—the middle of the eighteenth century—a good many Europeans and especially Englishmen were going to America to seek their fortunes. Robinson had left his wife and two children in York and set out to explore South America, in the hope of building up a profitable trade between England and Chile. A few weeks before, the *Virginia* had rounded the terrible Cape Horn. Now she was headed north for Valparaiso, which was Robinson's destination.

Robinson shuffled the cards. "Isn't this storm going to hold us up?" he asked the captain.

The captain stroked his tumbler of gin and looked at him with an ironic smile. With his long experience of the sea, he was amused at Robinson's youthful impatience.

"When you take a trip like this," he said, puffing at his pipe, "you start when you choose, but you get there when God chooses."

Then he removed the lid from his big tobacco jar and slipped his long china-bowl pipe into it. "In there," he explained, "it's protected from shocks and it drinks in the aroma of the tobacco."

He replaced the lid and leaned back lazily.

"You see," he said, "the advantage of storms is that they relieve you of all worry. Once the elements break loose, there's nothing you can do. So you do nothing. You put yourself in the hands of fate."

At that moment the lantern that lit the cabin gave a violent swing on its chain and shattered against the roof. Robinson barely had time to see the captain flying head first over the table. Then the cabin was plunged into darkness. Robinson stood up and was making for the door when a gust of wind told him that the door wasn't there any more. What frightened him most was that, after the rolling and pitching of the last few days, the ship wasn't moving at all. It must have run up on a reef or a sand bank. Great clouds were scudding over a full moon. In the dim light Robinson made out a group of men trying to lower a boat, and as he headed towards them to give them a hand, a violent tremor shook the whole ship. An instant later an enormous wave fell on the deck and swept away everything.

CHAPTER ONE

When Robinson recovered consciousness, he was lying with his face in the sand. A wave rolled over the wet beach and licked his feet. He turned over on his back. The sky was blue again after the storm, and black and white gulls were wheeling about. With a great effort Robinson sat up. He felt a sharp pain in his left shoulder. The beach was strewn with dead fish, broken shells, and black seaweed cast up by the waves. To the west a rocky promontory jutted into the sea, no doubt prolonged by a chain of reefs. And there lay the wreck of the *Virginia* with her masts uprooted and her halyards floating in the wind.

What was this unknown land? A continent, an island most probably? Was it inhabited? Were there other survivors like Robinson?

All these questions crossed his mind. Robinson stood up and took a few steps. No bones broken, but his bruised shoulder ached. The sun was getting hot, so he rolled a few of the big leaves that grew by the shore into a sort of

hat. Then he picked up a branch to use as a walking stick and ventured into the forest.

Felled trees, the dense underbrush and the lianas hanging from the branches formed an almost impenetrable tangle, and often Robinson had to crawl on all fours. The forest seemed deserted; there was not a sound to be heard. Suddenly Robinson started for he had caught sight of an animal perhaps a hundred yards ahead. It was a wild goat with very long shaggy hair. It stood there motionless and seemed to be watching him. Dropping his light stick, Robinson picked up a great knotted log to use as a club. When he came close, the goat lowered its head and made a dull grumbling sound. Robinson was seized with the fear that the goat was getting ready to charge. He raised his club and brought it down with all his might between the goat's horns. The beast fell to its knees, then rolled over on one side. The goat was not scared by Robinson but Robinson had been scared by the goat and he had killed the first living creature that he had met on the island.

After several hours, Robinson came to a hill formed of jagged boulders. There he found the entrance to a cave and went in, but before very long he decided the cave was too big to explore that day and turned back. He preferred to climb the hill and look about him. Standing on the highest boulder, he saw that there was water on all sides. He looked out over the country and found no sign of habitation, no sign of other survivors. So this was a desert island. That explained why the goat hadn't moved. Wild animals that have never seen a man before don't run at his approach. Their curiosity is aroused and they observe him.

This terrible discovery should have brought Robinson to the point of despair. But he was hungry and thirsty and this was not the time to complain. He began to search all around the big rock and soon he found some wild bananas and a fresh water spring. He ate with his knife and drank from the palm of his hand. Then he eased himself under the big stone and, overcome by fatigue and sadness, he fell asleep.

Awakened by the first rays of the sun, Robinson started back to the shore. Well rested after a good night's sleep, things didn't look so bad after all. True, the island seemed to be deserted. But wouldn't it be worse if it were inhabited by cannibals? Besides, it seemed rather a nice island, with its beautiful beach in the north, its wet and no doubt marshy meadows in the east, its great forest in the west and in the center that rocky hill, which not only offered a magnificent view on all sides, but also had a mysterious cave in it. In the midst of these thoughts, he came across the body of the wild goat he had killed. Half a dozen vultures with bare red necks and hooked beaks were fighting over it. Robinson swung his stick over his head and the great birds flew away one after another, running on their short crooked legs to take off. Then he loaded what was left of the goat on his back and, more slowly than before, went on to the beach. There he cut off one of the haunches, planted stakes in the ground wigwam shape, and hung the meat from the top. Then he made a fire under it. The crackling flames cheered him more than the meat, which was tough and had an unpleasantly strong taste. He decided to keep up the fire, partly to save his tinder box, and partly in the hope that a ship might come by and see it, though he realized that this was hardly necessary because any passing seafarers were sure to be attracted by the wreck of the *Virginia*. They would board it to see what they could find.

There were arms, tools and provisions in the hold. Perhaps, Robinson thought, he should save them before another tempest carried them away. But he still hoped this would be unnecessary because he felt sure that a ship would be coming along any minute. So he concentrated on setting up signals. He piled up branches and seaweed near the fire that was still burning; if a ship appeared on the horizon he would throw them into the fire and make great clouds of smoke. Then he had another idea. He could plant a pole in the ground, and to the top of it, fasten another pole crosswise, so that it would swing like a seesaw. If he sighted a ship, Robinson would attach a flaming brand to the end of the seesaw touching the ground and hoist it up by pulling down the other end by means of a liana. Later on, however, he would make something even better: On top of the cliff there was a big dead eucalyptus tree; its trunk was hollow. He stuffed the trunk with logs and kindling. When he set fire to them, they would in a few minutes turn the whole tree into a torch that could be seen for miles.

He ate whatever he happened to find: shell-fish, roots, coconuts, berries, birds' and turtles' eggs. The goat's carcass was beginning to smell. On the third day he hauled it away. But this he soon regretted for the vultures that had feasted on it kept following him about in the hope of another banquet. Sometimes they got on his nerves so much that he bombarded them with sticks and stones. Then the ugly things would fly lazily away but the next minute they were back again.

After a while Robinson got sick of watching the empty horizon. He decided to build a boat big enough to reach the coast of Chile. But that was impossible without tools. The idea didn't appeal to him, but he would just have to take what he needed from the *Virginia*. To reach the *Virginia,* he made a kind of raft by tying a dozen logs together with lianas. It wasn't a very good raft, but it would do if the sea were calm. The water wasn't deep so he propelled it with a long branch which touched bottom. He made two trips around the wreck. What he could see of the hull was intact; it must have been grounded on a hidden reef. If the crew had stayed below instead of exposing themselves on deck, they might all have been alive.

The deck was so cluttered with broken masts and tangled

spars and cables that he had a hard time getting through. The hold was in a disorderly state but at least it was dry. Robinson found chests full of biscuits and dried meat. He was hungry but he couldn't eat very much because he had nothing to drink. Of course, there were barrels of wine and spirits, but Robinson was a teetotaler; he had never touched a drop of alcohol and he wasn't going to begin now. His great surprise of the day was to discover, in the after-hold, forty kegs of black powder.

It took Robinson several days to carry all this powder ashore, because at high tide the water was too deep for him to use a branch. In between trips he built a shelter for it out of palm fronds weighted down with heavy stones. In addition to the powder, he brought back two cases of ship's biscuit, a spyglass, two flintlock muskets, a double-barreled pistol, two axes, a spade, a pick, a hammer, a bale of oakum, and an enormous piece of cheap red cloth intended for barter with any natives the *Virginia* might have come across. And in the captain's cabin he found the tobacco jar, still tightly closed. The fragile china-bowl pipe was undamaged. He tore a number of planks from the *Virginia's* decks and bulkheads and took them ashore. And finally in the mate's cabin he found a Bible which he wrapped carefully in a piece of sailcloth.

The very next day he started building a boat, which he hopefully christened the *Escape*.

CHAPTER TWO

Under the grass in a level clearing Robinson discovered a long straight tree trunk. Here was the keelson of his future boat. He started work at once, though still he kept watching the horizon in the hope of sighting a ship. First he lopped all the branches off the trunk, then he squared it. Though he had looked all over the *Virginia*, he had found neither nails nor screws, nor a drill, nor even a saw. He was obliged to dovetail the pieces together. He worked slowly and carefully, hardening the ends of the pieces with fire and then, after he had fitted them together, pouring water on the joints. The wood kept splitting and then he would have to remake the pieces, but he let nothing discourage him and he never felt tired.

What he missed most was a saw. A saw would have saved him months of hard work with ax and knife, but there was no way of making one with the materials at hand. One morning when he woke up he heard a sound which could only be that of someone sawing. He thought he must be dreaming. From time to time the sound stopped as if the workman had reached for a new log, then it started in again. Robinson crept slowly from his sleeping place under the rock and followed the sound. At first he saw nothing, then at the foot of a palm tree he caught sight of a giant crab holding a coconut in its claws and sawing at it. High up in the branches another crab was sending down the nuts by slicing their stems. Robinson's presence didn't seem to disturb the two crabs in the least; they went right on with their noisy work.

Robinson had no varnish or tar to caulk the hull with, but he knew how to make a kind of glue. It took him forty-five days. There was a clump of holly not far from the clearing. He cut most of it down and stripped off the outer bark. Then he removed the inner bark and cut it into strips. These he boiled in a kettle. Little by little they dissolved and formed a thick, sticky liquid which he spread, still boiling hot, over the hull of his boat.

When the *Escape* was finished, Robinson began to collect provisions for his voyage. But then he thought it might be wiser to launch his boat first and see how she acted in the water. Everything depended on this test, and he was afraid. He had been putting it off. Was the *Escape* seaworthy? Or would she capsize in the first wave? Robinson had nightmares about it. In the worst of them she no sooner touched the water than she sank straight to the bottom.

But finally he decided to go ahead. First of all he discovered that he was unable to slide the hull, which must have weighed half a ton, over the grass and sand. The fact is, he hadn't even stopped to think how he would move his boat to the shore. This was partly because he had been reading the Bible too much, especially the part about Noah's ark. Noah had built his ark far from the sea. He had simply waited for the waters to rise and come to him. Robinson had made a fatal mistake in not building the *Escape* directly on the beach.

He tried to slip rollers under the keel, but in vain; the hull wouldn't budge. He only stove in one of the side pieces with a log he was trying to use as a lever. After three days of useless effort, he was so tired and angry that he couldn't see straight. Then he thought of digging a trench from the sea to the boat. It would fill with water at high tide and he would only have to slide the boat into it. He started working. But the ground was stony under the surface and the job would take him at least ten years.

In midsummer the wild boars and their American cousins the peccaries spend the hottest hours of the day wallowing in the marshes. First they thrash about to stir up the muck with their paws, then they lie in the muddy water with only their heads sticking out. This protects them from the heat and the mosquitoes.

One day Robinson, discouraged by his failure with the *Escape*, followed a troop of peccaries and saw them vanish into their wallow. He was so tired and sad that he felt like doing the same. He took off his clothes and slipped into the fresh mud until only his eyes, nose and mouth rose above the surface. After that he spent whole days lying amidst the duckweed, water lilies and frogs' eggs. The gases rising from the stagnant water made him drowsy. Sometimes it seemed to him that he was at home in York; he heard the voices of his wife and children. Or he thought he was still a baby in his cradle, and the trees swaying in the wind were grown-ups bending over him.

In the evening when he tore himself out of the warm mud, his head was spinning. He was too weak to stand up, he could only walk on all fours, and he ate whatever came his way, with his nose to the ground like a pig. He never washed, and a crust of dried mud covered him from head to foot.

One morning as he was staggering toward his usual mire he heard something moving in a near bush. He stopped. His eyes crossed those of Tenn, the dog of the *Virginia*, with whom he had become friendly during the voyage. The animal had stopped still twelve feet from him, his ears pointed, left front foot bent forward. Robinson felt a warmth in his heart. This time he had proof that he was not the only one to escape from the wreck. He moved a few steps toward the animal and called him several times. The dog kept on the defense. Suddenly his lips tensed and he growled with hate. Then he turned around fast and ran away back into the bushes. Where did he disappear? Robinson did not attempt to follow him. He was too tired even to try to understand the behavior of his old friend. Had the dog gone back to a wild state? Had the terror and pain of shipwreck driven him to madness?

Another day when he was nibbling at a tuft of water-cress in a marshy pool, he thought he heard music. It was like a heavenly chorus, the voices of angels accompanied by chords on the harp. Robinson thought he was dead and that this was the music of Paradise. But raising his eyes, he saw a white sail on the horizon to the east. He dashed to his shipyard; his tools were lying about on the ground and he found his tinder box. Then he ran to the hollow eucalyptus, set fire to a bundle of dry branches, and pushed them through the hole in the tree trunk. A billow of acrid smoke poured out, but the fire didn't seem to take.

But what did it matter? He didn't need the fire. The ship was heading straight for the island. Soon it would drop anchor near the beach and send out a boat. Laughing like a madman, Robinson ran in all directions looking for trousers and a shirt. He finally found them under the hull of the *Escape*. Then, clawing at his face to disentangle his beard and hair which made him look like a wild animal, he ran down to the beach. The ship was very close now. Robinson saw her clearly, her sails leaning gracefully toward the white-crested waves. She was one of those Spanish galleons that used to cross the ocean, bringing gold, silver and gems from Mexico. As she came closer, Robinson saw a throng of splendidly dressed people on the deck. Some sort of celebration, he thought. On the quarter deck a small orchestra was playing and a chorus of children in white robes was singing. Couples were dancing a stately dance around a table covered with crystal and gold plates. No one seemed to see Robinson or even the shore along which the ship was sailing after coming about. Robinson ran along the beach after it. He shouted, waved his arms, stopped to pick up pebbles and threw them at the ship. He fell, picked himself up, fell again. The galleon was at the end of the beach where the dunes began. Robinson flung himself into the water and swam after it with all his might. Now he could only see the after-castle draped in brocade. A little girl was leaning out of a cabin window. She looked toward him and smiled sadly. Robinson knew her, he was sure of it. But who could she be? He opened his mouth to call out to her. Salt water poured into his throat. All he could see was the green water and a little skate speeding away from him backwards. . . .

Then he must have fainted. He was awakened by a pillar of flame. His teeth were chattering. Had the sea flung him a second time on the same stretch of beach? Up on the cliff the eucalyptus was blazing like a torch in the night. The signal fire had taken after all. Robinson staggered toward the light and heat.

He spent the rest of the night huddled up in the grass with his face toward the fire, moving closer as it died down. As the first light appeared in the sky, it came to him who the little girl on the galleon was. She was his own sister, Lucy, who had been dead for years. That meant the galleon hadn't been real. Of course not. The last galleon had disappeared from the seas more than two centuries ago. He was sick; he had been seeing things.

At last Robinson realized that lying in his mudhole and the pointless life he had been leading were driving him insane. The imaginary galleon was a warning. He would have to pull himself together.

Turning his back on the sea which had deceived him with its false hopes, he made for the forest and the rocky hill.

CHAPTER THREE

In the following weeks Robinson explored the island systematically, looking for springs and natural shelters, good places to fish, and clumps of coconut, pineapple and palm-cabbage trees. He set up his main storehouse in the cave under the rocky hill. Here he stored everything he was able to save from the wreck as a result of many trips back and forth before rough seas dislodged the hull from the reef and covered it completely. First the forty kegs of gunpowder, which he stowed away at the far end of the cave, then nearer the entrance, three chests full of clothing, five sacks of rice, wheat, barley and maize, two baskets of crockery and silverware, several boxes of odds and ends—candlesticks, spurs, jewels, magnifying glasses, spectacles, pen knives, sea charts, mirrors, dice, a case full of ship's cable, pulleys, fishing lines, floats, and so forth—and finally a strongbox full of silver and copper coins. The print on the books he found in the cabins had been almost washed away.

Robinson dried the white pages in the sun, planning to use them as a diary, if he could find something to use as ink.

Sea-porcupines are dangerous creatures with powerful jaws and poisonous bristles. When in danger, they blow themselves up like balloons and float on their backs, apparently in perfect bliss. One day Robinson found a number of these porcupine fish that had been washed up on the beach. He prodded one of them with a stick, and noticed that the tip was immediately stained a bright red and that the dye didn't wash off. He could use the red dye as ink! He cut himself a quill pen from a vulture's feather. Then he picked out the biggest of the washed and dried books to use as his diary and wrote his first words on paper. Every evening he would write down all the important things that had happened in the course of the day. On the first page of the book he drew a map of the island, and below the map he printed the word "Speranza" which means "hope," for that is what he decided to call the island, since he was determined never again to surrender to despair.

The most useful animals on the island were the goats, if only he could find a way to tame them. There were such quantities of them. It was easy enough to approach the mother goats, but they struggled fiercely when he tried to milk them. Robinson built a circular fence by driving stakes into the ground at intervals and tying saplings to them crosswise with vines. Into this enclosure he drove the young kids which attracted the mothers by their cries. When the mother goats were safe inside, he turned the kids out and waited for several days. By that time the goats' udders were swollen and painful, and they were only too willing to let themselves be milked.

When he inspected the sacks of rice, wheat, barley and maize which he had saved from the *Virginia*, he was in for a great disappointment. Some of the grain had been eaten by rats and weevils, with nothing left but husks mixed with droppings. Some had been spoiled by rain and sea water. Robinson was obliged to sort each sack grain by grain. It was hard, tiresome work, but when he had finished he had several pounds of seed. On another day he burned several acres of grassland. Then he broke up the soil with a spade, improvised from a piece of metal brought from the *Virginia* to which he had managed to attach a handle. Then he sowed crops of wheat, maize and barley.

Now Robinson had a herd of domestic animals and a tilled field. He had begun to tame the island. But time and again some incident reminded him that he was still living in a wild and hostile place. One morning he saw a vampire bat huddled over a kid, sucking its blood. These are giant bats with a wingspread of as much as thirty inches. At night they pounce, without so much as a sound, on the backs of sleeping animals and suck their blood. Another time, when Robinson was gathering shellfish on the half-submerged rocks, a stream of water hit him full in the face. Slightly dazed, he took a few steps but was stopped by a second squirt. He looked around and finally discovered a little gray squid hidden away between the rocks. This animal had the astonishing gift of shooting jets of water from its mouth and aiming them with remarkable precision.

One day when Robinson had broken his spade and let his best milk goat get away, he felt so discouraged that he went back to the mudhole. He took off his clothes and slipped into the warm mud. Clouds of mosquitoes swarmed around his head and he breathed in the poisonous vapors rising from the water. He lost all sense of time and place. He was a child again in York, he heard he voices of his parents and of his brothers and sisters. The next day he realized that his most dangerous enemies were laziness and discouragement and that his only hope was to keep as busy as possible.

The maize was a total failure; the field where he had planted it was soon overgrown with nettles and thistles. But the barley and wheat throve. As he stroked the tender young shoots he felt, for the first time since he had been on Speranza, a surge of happiness. When the time came to harvest his crop, he looked about for something to use as a scythe and finally found an old boarding cutlass that the captain of the *Virginia* had had hanging on the wall of his cabin. First he tried to mow at a slow, steady pace as he had seen the peasants do at home. But as he was handling this warlike weapon he was seized by a strange frenzy. He slashed through the field shouting furious battle cries. His strange method of reaping didn't spoil too much of the grain, but it ruined the straw, which was hacked to pieces, scattered and trampled.

He threshed the grain by beating it with a stick, and winnowed it by pouring it from one basket into another in the wind, which sent the husks and chaff whirling far away. When he had finished he found that his harvest came to thirty pecks of wheat and twenty of barley, and he felt very proud. To make flour he had prepared a mortar and pestle —a hollowed-out tree trunk and a thick branch rounded at one end. The oven—carved in the soft stone in a wall of the cave—was ready for the first baking. But then suddenly he decided not to make the bread yet, but to use his whole harvest for seed. In going without bread, he thought he was being virtuous and sensible. Actually he was developing a new vice, *avarice*, which was to do him a great deal of harm.

Not long after the first harvest, to Robinson's great joy, Tenn, the *Virginia's* dog, turned up again. He suddenly appeared from nowhere, wriggling and whimpering with joy and licking Robinson's hands. Robinson never found out how the dog had lived all this time on the island. He understood that at the time of his first meeting with the dog it had been his fierce aspect and his dirty appearance which caused the animal to run away. He remembered stories he had heard of dogs compelled in spite of their own feeling of attachment to leave a master who had become an alcoholic or run so low that he ate from the same bowl. Tenn's comeback was a proof that he was in the process of becoming civilized once more.

Now that his trusted friend had come back, he decided to carry out a plan he had been turning over in his mind

for a long time: to build a real house. He was sick of sleeping in the cave or under a tree. After choosing a spot near
the big cedar tree in the middle of the island, he dug a rec-
tangular trench to keep out the moisture and covered the
bottom first with a layer of pebbles, then with a layer of
white sand. On this foundation he built walls of palm logs.
The roof was made of reeds, covered with the leaves of
rubber plants placed in overlapping rows like slates. He
plastered the outer walls of the house with a mortar of clay
and dried straw. Over the sand floor of the house he laid
flat irregular stones which he fitted together like a puzzle.
Goat skins and reed mats, a few pieces of furniture that
Robinson had made of osier, the dishes and lanterns, the
spyglass, and finally the saber and one of the muskets which
he hung up on the wall gave the house a comfortable, home-
like atmosphere that was a welcome change for Robinson.
He unpacked the clothes chests he had brought ashore—
some of the things were really magnificent—and soon got
into the habit of dressing for dinner in jacket, breeches,
shoes and stockings.

After a time he noticed that from inside the house the
sun could be seen only at certain hours. He decided that a
clock would come in handy; then he would be able to tell
what time it was at any hour of the day or night. After
several unsuccessful experiments, he succeeded in making
a *clepsydra*, a kind of water clock that people used long ago.
It consisted of a large glass jug—brought from the *Virginia*—with a small hole in the bottom. The jug was filled

with water which fell drop by drop into a copper basin. It took the jug twenty-four hours to empty. On the outside Robinson had scratched twenty-four parallel circles, each marked with a number. The water level indicated the hour. He also needed a calendar to tell him what day of the week and what month it was and how many years had passed. But he had no idea how much time he had spent on the island. A year, two years? Or even more? He decided to start at zero. In front of his house he set up a calendar pole—a tree trunk from which the bark had been stripped. Each day he made a little notch in it and each month a deeper notch. After the twelfth month he would make a large figure ONE, indicating the first year of his local calendar.

CHAPTER FOUR

The days passed. Robinson was still worried about the mudhole. It would be so easy to lie down in it and let himself turn into an animal. It's hard to live like a human being without anyone to help you. He came to the conclusion that the only way was to work harder and harder, developing the resources of the island, and to keep a very strict schedule.

When he had notched up a thousand days on his calendar, he decided that Speranza needed laws and that it was up to him to make them. He put on a dress uniform and stationed himself at his high desk which he had built that way because he liked to write standing up. Then he opened the grandest of his sea-washed volumes and wrote:

Charter of Speranza Island
begun on the one-thousandth day of the local calendar

ARTICLE I. *Robinson Crusoe, born in York on De-cember 19, 1737, is appointed Governor of Sper-*

anza Island situated in the Pacific Ocean between the Juan Fernando Islands and the coast of Chile. By virtue of his office, he is empowered to draw up laws for the island and its territorial waters.

ARTICLE II. *The inhabitants of the island are required to think out loud.*

(With no one to talk to, Robinson was afraid of forgetting how to speak. Even now, when he tried, his tongue felt muddled as if he had drunk too much wine. But with the new law he would have to talk all the time, to the trees, to the stones, to the clouds, and, of course, to Tenn and the goats.)

ARTICLE III. *Friday is a day of fasting.*

ARTICLE IV. *Sunday is a day of rest. At seven o'clock on Saturday evening all work on the island must cease and the inhabitants must put on their best clothes for dinner. At ten o'clock on Sunday morning they must gather in the temple for prayer.*

(In making these laws Robinson had to pretend that the island had many inhabitants, for it seemed silly to make laws just for one man. Besides, he hoped that some day a companion, or perhaps even several companions, would turn up.)

ARTICLE V. *Only the Governor is authorized to smoke a pipe. But only once a week, on Sunday, after lunch.*

He had only recently discovered the pleasure of smoking Captain Van Deyssel's china-bowl pipe. Unfortunately, his supply of tobacco wouldn't last forever, and he wanted to make it stretch as long as possible.

But what would be the punishment for breaking these laws? Robinson decided to stop work and give the matter a little thought. He went to the door and opened it wide. How beautiful his island was! The foliage was like a green sea ruffled by the wind and merging in the distance with the green line of the ocean. The sky overhead was perfectly blue and cloudless. No! It wasn't perfectly blue! There was a cloud of smoke over the beach. Robinson was sure he hadn't left any fires burning. Could there be visitors? He took a musket, a powder horn, a bag of show and his spyglass. Then he whistled for Tenn and plunged into the woods, avoiding the direct path leading from the cave to the shore.

Three long outrigger canoes were drawn up on the dry sand. Some forty men were standing in a circle around a fire which sent up a column of dense white smoke. Robinson studied them through his spyglass. They were short and thickset, dressed in crude leather aprons. They had broad faces and their eyes were unusually far apart. But strangest of all, they had no eyebrows. They had plucked them out. They had long black hair which they tossed in proud defiance at the slightest pretext. Robinson recognized them as Araucanians, a savage and warlike tribe of Indians who lived on the coast of Chile. In times gone by they had held

the Inca invaders at bay and had inflicted bloody defeats on the Spanish Conquistadores. Robinson knew that they would show no mercy for any white man.

Had they made the long crossing from Chile to Speranza in their canoes? It was possible, they were known to be great sailors. But it seemed more likely that they had set up a colony on one of the Juan Fernandez Islands. Lucky for him, Robinson thought, that he hadn't been cast ashore there, for they would certainly have made a slave of him, or perhaps even massacred him.

Because of the stories he had heard in their country, he was able to guess the meaning of the ceremony they were performing on the beach. The men formed a circle and inside it a bony old woman with wild, waving hair was staggering back and forth. She went to the fire and threw a handful of some sort of powder into it. A billow of dense white smoke went up, and she breathed it in avidly. Then she turned toward the motionless Indians and seemed to pass them in review. She moved about, stopping in front of one, then another. Then she went back to the fire and started all over again.

She was a sorceress. There had been some misfortune—a member of the tribe had fallen sick or died . . . or perhaps there had been a fire, a storm, or a poor harvest. One of the Indians must be to blame and she was going to find out which one it was. Suddenly her bony arm shot out toward one of the men and angry howls poured from her mouth. Trembling with fear, the Indian she had pointed out threw himself on the ground. One of the others raised his machete and sent the apron flying. Then he brought the machete down in regular blows, cutting off the victim's head, arms and legs. The six pieces were then thrown into the fire and the smoke turned black.

The Indians broke their circle and made for the canoes. Six of them took water skins and went into the woods. Robinson slipped away but kept his eye on the invaders of his domain. If they detected signs of life on the island, they might come looking for him and he would have a hard time escaping. Luckily there was a water hole at the edge of the forest so there was no need for the Indians to go any further. They filled their skins, slung them on poles—two men to a pole—and went back to the canoes. The others had already taken their places. The sorceress sat huddled on a kind of throne at the stern of one of the canoes.

When the canoes had disappeared behind the cliffs, Robinson approached the fire. He could still make out the charred remains of the man who had been so cruelly sacrificed because an old sorceress held him responsible for some calamity. With his heart full of fear, disgust and sadness, Robinson went back to his governor's mansion and resumed his work of writing the laws of Speranza.

ARTICLE VI. *The Island of Speranza is declared to be a fortified place. Its commander is the governor who holds the rank of general. A curfew will go into effect one hour after sunset.*

In the following months, the constant fear of a return visit by the Araucanians had kept Robinson busy building a wall equipped with firing slits around his house and the entrance to the cave. Outside the wall he dug a moat seven feet wide and ten feet deep. The two muskets and the pistol were kept ready loaded, their muzzles protruding from the three middle slits. That would prevent the enemy from guessing that the fort had only one defender. The boarding cutlass and the ax were also within easy reach, but it seemed unlikely that there would ever be hand-to-hand fighting because Robinson had set snares all around the moat. First there were staggered rows of pits covered with grass held up by thin reed matting. Anyone who stepped on the grass would fall on a pointed stake planted in the bottom of the pit. At the edge of the forest, where the enemy might be expected to assemble before the attack, he buried two kegs of powder, to which he attached a fuse that could be lit within the fortress. In addition, the moat could only be crossed by a bridge that could be raised from inside the fort.

Every night before sounding the curfew on his horn, Robinson made his rounds, followed by Tenn who seemed to be aware of the danger threatening Speranza and its inhabitants. Then he closed the fortress. Great boulders had been placed in such a way that any attackers would have to pass over the pits. The bridge was drawn up and the entrances barricaded. Then Robinson sounded curfew, made dinner, set the table and withdrew to the cave. A few minutes later he came out washed and combed, his beard trimmed, and wearing his general's uniform. In the light of candles consisting of sticks coated with resin, he slowly ate his dinner under the watchful and devoted eyes of Tenn.

CHAPTER FIVE

A period of heavy rains followed. The house, the pathways and enclosures had been damaged by the downpour, and Robinson was kept busy making repairs. When the rains had stopped and the sun had dried the land, it was time to harvest the grain. There was so much of it that Robinson had to clean out another cave not far from the large one. This time Robinson did not deny himself the pleasure of baking some bread, the first he had eaten since he had been stranded on the island.

The abundance of grain soon made it necessary to do something about the rats, which seemed to grow in proportion to the food supply. Robinson believed that certain white mushrooms with red spots must be poisonous, because several kids had died after nibbling bits of them along with their grass. He gathered as many as he could find, boiled them and made a yellowish brew in which he soaked some grains of wheat. Then he put the poisoned grains in the usual paths of the rats. They gobbled them up and were not even sick. Then he made cages with trap doors. But he would have needed thousands of cages, and besides, once he had caught the rats he had to drown them, and he couldn't bear to lower the cages into the water and watch the animals die.

One day Robinson saw two rats having a furious fight. Blind and deaf to everything around them, they rolled on the ground squeaking angrily. In the end they bit into each other's throats and died without unlocking their jaws. Robinson saw that the two rats were not of the same breed. One was black, plump and short-haired like the rats he had often seen on board ship. The other was gray, with a longer body and thick fur. He had seen others just like it in the fields of the island. Robinson realized that the black rats came from the *Virginia* and had multiplied thanks to his stores of grain, while the gray ones had always lived on the island. Each variety seemed to have its own territory. To make sure of this, Robinson caught a rat in the cave and let it loose in the meadow. For some time the quivering grass was the only sign that a merciless chase was going on. Then Robinson saw a flurry of sand at the foot of a dune. When he got to it he found there was nothing left of the black rat but a few shreds of skin and hair.

He strewed two sacks of grain over the meadow. Then he went from the meadow to the cave, dropping grain to make a trail. This was a heavy sacrifice for Robinson and he wasn't even sure it would succeed. But it did. At nightfall the black rats came out in hordes to bring back the grain which they seemed to regard as their property. The gray rats massed to repulse the sudden invasion. Soon they were locked in battle. It looked as though a storm were raising little spouts of sand all over the meadow. Pairs of rats in single combat rolled over and over like living balls, and angry squeaks were heard on all sides.

An animal fighting in enemy territory is almost always defeated. That day all the black rats were killed.

Robinson was opposed to personal vanity, and it had been ages since he had really stopped to look at himself. Then one day he rummaged around in one of the sea chests and pulled out a mirror. He was quite startled to see his face. Actually he hadn't changed so very much, except that his beard was longer and he noticed a few new wrinkles around his eyes. But his face looked so stiff and sad. He tried very hard to raise the corners of his mouth to make a smile, but he couldn't. He had forgotten how to smile! It was as if his face had become a wooden mask with a dreary expression that never changed. He had been alone too long! There had been no one to smile at in such a long time that when he tried, his muscles refused to obey. He stared at the hard, stern face in the glass and felt very sad. He had everything he needed on his island, he had plenty to eat and drink, he had a house and a bed to sleep in. The only thing he lacked was someone to smile at.

Then he looked down at Tenn. Was he dreaming? *The dog was smiling at him!* His black upper lip was raised on one side, uncovering two rows of teeth. At the same time he cocked his head to one side in an odd way and screwed up his hazel colored eyes. Robinson took the great shaggy head in both hands and his eyes filled with tears. Suddenly he felt a slight trembling at the corners of his mouth. Tenn kept smiling and Robinson, in his eagerness to learn to smile again, kept on smiling at him.

After that it was like a game between them. Robinson would stop whatever he was doing—working, hunting or walking on the beach—and stare at Tenn in a special way. The dog would smile at him in *his* special way, and little by little Robinson's face would grow soft and human. He too was smiling.

CHAPTER SIX

Robinson never stopped civilizing and putting order into his island. From day to day he had more work; he created new responsibilities for himself. In the morning he washed and dressed and then read a few pages of the Bible. Next he ran up the flag and, standing at attention, saluted it. Then he opened the fortress. He lowered the drawbridge over the moat and removed the boulders from the entrances. The morning's work began with the milking of the goats, followed by an inspection of the rabbit warren he was trying to develop. In a sandy clearing he was raising a crop of wild turnips, lucerne, and oats in the hope of attracting an *agoutis*—a variety of plump, long-legged, short-eared Chilean hare—that were scattered over the island.

A little later he checked the water level of the fresh-water fish pools. At noon he had a quick meal with Tenn and took a short nap, after which he put on his general's uniform to attend to his official duties. He took a census of the sea turtles, each of which he had marked with a serial number, and presided over the opening of a bridge of lianas flung boldly over a ravine a hundred feet deep in the middle of the woods. Then he had to finish building a hut of tree ferns at the edge of the forest not far from the bay. It would be an excellent observation post offering a wide view of the sea, and would also be a cool place in which to rest during the heat of the day.

Often Robinson felt crushed under the weight of his work and official duties. What use was it all? But then he remembered the mudhole and the dangers of idleness and began to work harder than ever.

For a long time Robinson had used the main cave for storing his most precious possessions: near the entrance his stocks of grain, his preserved fruit and salted meat; behind them his chests of clothing, his tools, weapons and gold; and farthest back his kegs of powder, which would have been enough to blow up the whole island. He hadn't hunted with firearms in a long while, but he was glad to have all that powder; it made him feel safer and gave him a sense of superiority.

He had never explored the deepest part of the cave and sometimes he felt curious about it. Behind the kegs of powder there was a narrow, steeply sloping tunnel, and one day he decided to see where it led.

There was one main difficulty: how would he be able to see where he was going? He had nothing to make a light with but torches of resinous wood. But if he went deep into the cave with a torch, there was a risk of setting fire to the powder, especially as he might have spilled some on the ground when he had moved the kegs. In addition such torches make so much smoke that he would be unable to breathe. For a time he thought of sinking a shaft into the cave to let in light and air, but the rock was too hard. In the end there seemed to be only one solution: he must learn to get used to the darkness. Providing himself with a few maize cakes and a jug of goat's milk, he went in as far as he could and waited. There was not a sound to be heard. He knew that the sun was dropping toward the horizon. Since the mouth of the cave faced west, Robinson felt sure that for a moment the setting sun would shine straight into the tunnel and light up the whole cave. And that is exactly what happened. He took a quick look about him. Then the light went out and he knew that his first day had ended.

He went to sleep, woke up, ate a cake, drank some milk and went back to sleep. Then suddenly another flash. Twenty-four hours had elapsed, but for Robinson they had passed like a dream. He was losing his sense of time. The next twenty-four hours passed even more quickly, and Robinson no longer knew whether he was asleep or awake.

At length he decided to get up and go deeper into the cave. He groped about a bit and finally found what he was looking for: the opening of a narrow vertical passage. He tried to slip into it. The walls were perfectly smooth but the hole was so small that his hips would not go through. He took off his clothes and rubbed himself with the sour milk that was left at the bottom of the jug. Then he plunged into

[43]

the opening head first. This time he slipped through slowly but steadily.

He landed gently in a niche just big enough to hold him if he doubled up. The air was strangely warm. He drew his knees up to his chin, crossed his ankles, rested his hands on his feet, and settled down. He was so comfortable that he fell asleep. When he awoke, he was amazed to find that the darkness around him had turned white. He still couldn't see anything but before his eyes there was no blackness; everything was white. The hole he was in was so warm and cosy and white that he began to think about his mother. He thought he was in her arms and that she was rocking him and singing softly. His father was a small, sickly man, but his mother was a big woman, strong and calm. She never got angry, but she only had to look at her children to know what they had been up to.

One day when she was upstairs with her children and the father was away, fire had broken out in the shop on the ground floor. The house, which was very old, was built of wood, and the flames spread quickly. The little draper, Robinson's father, saw the flames as he was returning home. He ran about outside the house wailing that his wife and children were being burned alive. And then he saw his wife step calmly out of a sea of flames and smoke. She had all her children with her, on her back, on her shoulders, in her arms, or clinging to her apron. That was how Robinson saw her now—like a tree bending under the weight of its fruit.

He shook himself. He knew he'd better hurry up and get

out of the hole if he didn't want to stay there forever. He barely managed to hoist himself through the passage. Then he groped about and found his clothes, which he rolled up in a ball. The darkness around him was still white and that frightened him. Had he gone blind? He staggered to the mouth of the cave and suddenly the sunlight hit him full in the face. It was the hottest hour of the day, the hour when even the lizards look for shade. But Robinson was so cold that his teeth were chattering. Burying his face in his hands, he made his way to the house. Tenn frisked for joy at his master's appearance, but he was upset at seeing him naked and so weak.

CHAPTER SEVEN

Several times Robinson went back to the hole in the cave to find the wonderful peace of his childhood. But he was troubled. Could it be laziness that made him go there, the same laziness that had driven him to lie in the mudhole?

To cheer himself up he decided to plant the rice he had been saving since he came to the island. He had kept putting it off because he knew that laying out a rice paddy meant months of back-breaking toil. Rice has to grow under water, and the water level has to be regulated. He would have to build two dams in a brook, one downstream to flood the meadow that was to be his paddy, and another upstream that would enable him to drain the paddy. He would need dikes and sluices that could be opened and closed as required. In ten months, if all went well, the harvesting and husking of the rice would require days of hard work.

But then when the paddy was finished and he had sowed the rice, Robinson started to wonder again: Why was he working his fingers to the bone? If he hadn't been alone, if he had had a wife and children, or even a single human companion, he would have known what he was working for. But all alone like this, it seemed so useless.

With tears in his eyes he went back to the cave. This time he stayed so long that he was almost too weak to climb out again. When he finally did, he realized that he might have died down there in his hole. There must be something, he thought, that would give him the courage to live like a man and go on working.

Then he remembered a book his father had given him to read when he was a boy. The book was *Poor Richard's Almanack*, by Benjamin Franklin. Benjamin Franklin believed that a man's most important duty was to work. The book contained many wise sayings and words of advice. It seemed to Robinson that if he wrote these sayings all over the island so as to have them before his eyes wherever he went, they would help him to fight his discouragement and laziness. With sticks arranged to form letters in the sand he wrote such sentences as: "Poverty robs a man of all virtue: it is hard for an empty sack to stand upright."

In one of the walls of the cave he set little stones that spelled out:

"If lying is the second vice, the first is indebtedness: for lies ride on the back of debts."

In a bed of stones he placed pine logs wrapped in oakum ready to be lighted, and they were so arranged as to read:

"If knaves knew all the advantages of virtue, they would turn virtuous out of knavery."

One of these sayings was longer than the rest. It had 113 letters. Robinson hit on the idea of clipping these letters into the hair of the goats in his enclosure, a letter to each goat. Once in a blue moon the goats might, in moving about, arrange the 113 letters in such a way as to spell out the saying, which was:

"He who kills a cow destroys her progeny unto the thousandth generation; he who squanders a crown piece destroys a mountain of sovereigns."

Robinson was about to start to work when suddenly he started with surprise and fear. He had seen a wisp of white smoke rising in the blue sky. It came from the same place as before. But this time the Indians were sure to see his letters in the sand and know that someone was here. Cursing himself for his weird ideas, he ran for the fort followed by Tenn. Then something happened that struck him as a bad omen: frightened by all the excitement, one of his billy goats, ordinarily a tame, good natured animal, lowered his horns and charged him. Robinson barely managed to get out of the way, but the goat struck Tenn and tossed him, howling for all he was worth, into a clump of ferns.

Robinson rolled the boulders into place at the entrances, pulled up the drawbridge, and shut himself up in the fort with Tenn. But then he wondered whether this was the sensible thing to do. If the Indians detected his presence and decided to attack the fort, they would have the advantage not only of numbers but of surprise as well. On the other hand, perhaps they were not interested in him, but only in their murderous ceremonies. What a relief that would be! He decided to find out. He took one of the muskets, slipped the pistol into his belt, and started through the

[49]

woods in the direction of the shore. Though bruised and limping, Tenn followed along. When Robinson had gone a short way, it occurred to him that his spyglass might come in handy and he went back to get it.

There were again three outrigger canoes drawn up on the beach. The circle around the fire was larger than the first time, and when Robinson looked at them through his spyglass it seemed to him that they were not the same group. One poor Indian had already been chopped up. Two warriors had just stepped away from the fire into which they had thrown the pieces. Then a strange thing happened. The sorceress, who was squatting on the ground, suddenly jumped up and ran to one of the men. She pointed her bony arm at him, opened her mouth wide, and poured out a flood of curses. She had chosen a second victim! For a time, the Indians hesitated. Then the marked man's two neighbors picked him up and threw him to the ground, while a third man came toward him brandishing a machete. The machete descended and the victim's leather apron flew into the air. It would have fallen on the man's naked body, but he leapt to his feet and bounded towards the woods. In Robinson's spyglass he seemed to be jumping up and down in one place with two other Indians close behind him. Actually he was running with amazing speed—straight toward Robinson. He was no taller than the others but much more slender, with the build of a runner. His skin seemed darker than theirs. Perhaps the sorceress had found him guilty because he was different from the rest of the group.

He was coming closer by the second and his lead over the

others kept growing. Robinson was sure he himself could not be seen from the beach or he would have thought the Indian was coming to him for protection. He had to make a decision. In a moment the three Indians would see him. Perhaps they would make up and join forces against him. Just then Tenn started barking furiously in the direction of the beach. Stupid dog! Robinson rushed at him and gripped the dog's muzzle in his left hand, while with his right he shouldered his musket. By killing one of the pursuers he risked the danger of having a whole tribe against him. By killing the fugitive he was fulfilling the ritual execution. Wisdom suggested that he be on the stronger side. He aimed at the chest of the fugitive who was no more than thirty feet from him. As he fired, Tenn jumped on one side trying to free himself. Robinson missed and, to his surprise, it was the first of two pursuers who was thrown back and fell on the sand. The other stopped, bent down over the body of his companion, then stood up, looked through the curtain of branches beyond which one could see the beach and finally ran back like mad toward the group of the other Indians.

The victim was cowering in a clump of dwarf palms. He crawled over to Robinson, touched his head to the ground, and groped for Robinson's foot which he placed on his own neck in token of submission.

Robinson and the Indian spent the night in the fort, listening intently for any unusual sound. Every two hours Robinson sent Tenn out on reconnaissance. The dog would bark if he saw or smelled any invaders. Each time he came

back without barking an alarm. The Indian, now wearing an old pair of sailor's trousers which Robinson had made him put on, was dejected and listless. His narrow escape from death seemed to have left him dazed and perhaps he was bewildered by the strange place he had been brought to. He wouldn't touch the wheat cake Robinson had given him but kept chewing some kind of wild beans. Just before daybreak the Indian fell asleep on a pile of dry leaves, holding the sleeping dog in his arms. It was surprising how Tenn, who was rather suspicious by nature, put up with it.

Maybe the Indians were waiting for daylight to attack. Armed with the two muskets, the pistol, and as much powder and shot as he could carry, Robinson slipped out of the fort and, making a long detour through the dunes, went down to the shore.

The beach was deserted. The three canoes had disappeared. The body of the Indian Robinson had shot the day before had been taken away. Nothing was left but a circle of charred logs and blackened bones, where the magic fire had been. Hopefully, the Indians had interpreted the killing as another act of supernatural fate and would be afraid to return. Robinson put his arms and ammunition down on the beach with an enormous feeling of relief. For a long time he was shaken with a wild nervous laughter. When he stopped to catch his breath, it came to him that this was his first laugh since the shipwreck. Could it be that he was able to laugh again because at last he had company? Suddenly he had an idea and he broke into a run. The *Escape!* He had always kept away from his shipyard. His failure to launch his boat had been a cruel disappointment and he didn't like to be reminded of it. But, he thought, the little boat must still be there waiting for arms strong enough to haul it to the beach. Perhaps the two of them together would succeed, and then the Indian's knowledge of the islands would come in very handy.

As he approached the fort, Robinson saw the Indian all naked, playing with Tenn. He was annoyed at the savage's lack of modesty and also at the friendship that seemed to have sprung up between him and Tenn. After making him put on the trousers, which were much too big for him, Robinson led him to the *Escape*.

The whole clearing was overgrown with gorse, and the little boat seemed to be floating in a sea of yellow flowers. The mast had fallen and there were bulges in the deck, caused no doubt by the humidity, but the hull seemed to be in good shape. Tenn who was running ahead gambolled about the boat. Then he crouched down and jumped up on the deck. It caved in under his weight and Robinson saw him disappear into the hold howling with fright. Every time Tenn tried to escape from his prison, another section of the deck would collapse. The Indian put his hand on the gunwale, closed it and opened it again under the astonished eyes of Robinson: it was full of a fine red dust that scattered in the wind. The Indian burst out laughing. Robinson kicked the hull gently: a great hole opened up in the side of the boat and a cloud of dust arose. The termites had made a meal of the *Escape*. She was beyond repair.

CHAPTER EIGHT

For a long time Robinson wondered what to call the Indian. He couldn't very well give him a Christian name until he had been baptized. Finally he decided to name him after the day on which he had found him. And so the second occupant of the island was called Friday.

Robinson taught Friday English. His method was simple. He showed him a daisy and said: "Daisy."

And Friday repeated: "Daisy."

Robinson corrected his pronunciation when necessary. Then he showed him a goat, a knife, a parrot, the sun, a cheese, a mirror, a brook, saying slowly: "Goat, knife, parrot, sun, cheese, mirror, brook."

Friday said the words after him, and repeated them until he could say them properly.

In a few months Friday knew enough English to understand Robinson's orders and name all the useful things around them. He also learned to clear ground, plow, sow, harrow, transplant, hoe, mow, reap, thresh, grind flour, knead dough and bake bread. He learned to milk the goats, make cheese, gather turtles' eggs and make an omelet out of them, to mend Robinson's clothes and shine his boots. He had become a model servant. In the evening he put on servant's livery and waited on the governor's table. After dinner he warmed his master's bed with an iron kettle full of coals. Then, his work done, he put down a bundle of straw outside the house door and there he and Tenn slept.

Robinson was happy because at last he had someone to work for him; someone to whom he could teach civilization. After a while Friday knew that whatever his master ordered him to do was good and whatever he forbade was bad. It was bad to eat more than the portion Robinson gave him. It was bad to smoke the pipe, to go about naked, or to hide away and sleep when there was work to do. Friday had learned to be a soldier when his master was the general, a choir boy when his master prayed, a mason when he was building, a porter when he went on a journey, and a beater when he hunted; and he had learned to chase the flies away with a palm frond when his master was taking a nap.

Robinson had still another reason to be pleased. Now he knew what to do with the coins he had saved from the *Virginia*. He paid Friday: half a gold sovereign a month. With his wages Friday bought extra food and knickknacks from the *Virginia's* stores, or half a day's rest—he was not allowed to buy a full day. He spent a good deal of his free time lying in a hammock he had slung between two trees.

Sunday of course was the best day in the week. In the

morning the servant brought the governor a kind of cane which looked like a cross between a king's scepter and a bishop's crozier. Then, shaded by a goat skin parasol carried by Friday who walked behind him, Robinson would stride along majestically, inspecting his fields, his rice paddies and orchards, his flocks and his new buildings. He distributed praise and blame, gave orders for the following week, and drew up plans for the years to come. Then it would be time for dinner, which would be more carefully prepared and more copious than during the week. Friday would spend the afternoon cleaning up and beautifying the island. He would clean the paths, plant flowers in front of the house, and prune the ornamental trees.

Friday often had good ideas that won his master's approval. One of Robinson's biggest worries was how to get rid of the waste from his kitchen and workshop without attracting vultures or rats. If he buried the waste, the rats would dig it up. If he threw it in the sea, the tide would throw it back on the beach. He didn't like to burn it because of the foul-smelling smoke which clung to the house and his clothes.

Friday discovered a colony of large red ants near the house. His idea was to deposit the waste on the huge ant hill. In one moment it was covered with ants and in the next moment it was gone—not a thing left but clean, bare bones.

Friday also taught Robinson how to use the *bola*. A *bola* is a weapon much used in South America, consisting of three round stones fastened to thongs joined in a knot.

When it is thrown in the right way the thongs spin like the spokes of a wheel. When they hit something that is not too big they wrap themselves around it and hold it fast.

Friday would throw his *bola* at the goats and catch them by the legs when he wanted to milk them. He showed Robinson how to use it for capturing deer and long-legged birds. And he explained that if bigger stones were used the *bola* became a terrible weapon that could crush a man's chest and half strangle him. Robinson who was always fearful of another invasion of Indians, was grateful for this silent, deadly weapon that was so easy to make. They spent long hours practicing on the beach, using a tree trunk the size of a man for a target.

Another of Friday's ideas was to make a canoe of the type used in his country. He chose a thick, straight pine trunk and hollowed it out with an ax. He worked slowly and patiently. There was no sign of the feverish haste with which Robinson had built the *Escape*. Still smarting under his failure, Robinson took no part in the work but merely looked on. After rough-hewing his canoe, Friday smoothed it inside and out with a pocket knife.

When it was finished, the canoe was so light that Friday could lift it up and hold it over his head. With Tenn bounding about him, he carried it down to the beach and launched it. Robinson, in a very bad humor, followed at a distance. But when he saw the little boat bouncing on the waves, he forgot his jealousy. He got in behind Friday and picked up one of the paddles the Indian had carved from an araucaria branch. For the first time they made the circuit of the island by sea. Tenn bounded along the beach beside them, barking.

Everything seemed to be going well. The island was thriving, with its tilled fields, its flocks, its orchards and the new buildings that went up week after week. Friday worked hard and Robinson governed. Tenn, who was growing old, took longer and longer naps.

Actually, all three of them were bored. Friday was obedient out of gratitude. He wanted to please Robinson who had saved his life. But he didn't understand all this organization, all these rules and ceremonies; he didn't even see the point of the cultivated fields, domestic animals and houses. Robinson told him this was what people did in the civilized countries of Europe, but Friday didn't see why they had to do the same thing on a desert island in the Pacific. Robinson understood how Friday felt. And he also knew that although the Indian did his best, there was no telling what he might do as soon as he had a moment or two of freedom.

Friday's feeling about animals was a mystery to Robinson. To Robinson's way of thinking, animals were either useful or harmful; useful animals should be protected and allowed to multiply, harmful ones must be destroyed. Friday didn't see it that way at all. He would pick out some animal to make friends with, and he didn't care in the least whether his new friend was useful or not.

He took it into his head to tame a pair of rats, and even Tenn learned to leave these creatures alone because Friday had taken them under his wing. Robinson was determined to get rid of them but it wasn't so easy. He took them out in the canoe and threw them into the sea. The rats swam ashore and came right back to the house. He took them out in the canoe again, but this time he tricked them. Instead of throwing them in the water, he put them on a board. The rats, afraid to jump overboard, clung to their raft and the current carried them out to sea. Friday didn't say a word, but Robinson could see that he knew what had happened, as though Tenn had told him all about it.

Another day Friday disappeared for several hours. Robinson was about to set out in search of him when, looking out in the direction of the beach, he saw a column of smoke. There was no law against making fires on the island, but there was a rule that anyone wishing to make a fire must give the governor advance notice and tell him when and where the fire was going to be made. That way Robinson would not think the Araucanians were back whenever he saw smoke. It was clear to Robinson that since Friday hadn't given notice, he must be up to something his master wouldn't approve of. With a sigh Robinson started for the beach.

Friday was hard at work. At first Robinson couldn't make out what he was doing. Then he saw that he had placed a huge turtle upside down on a bed of coals. The turtle, not yet dead, was thrashing the air furiously with its four paws. Robinson thought he heard a hoarse cough. That must have been the turtle's way of crying out. Torturing a poor turtle! Robinson was disgusted. He began to have a glimmer of what was going on when he saw the shell flatten out and come loose from the turtle's body. Friday cut the ligaments that still stuck to the shell and instantly the turtle rolled free of the shell. It scrambled down the beach, followed by Tenn who ran after it barking. A moment later it had disappeared into the waves.

"Silly turtle," said Friday calmly. "The crabs will eat it up."

The shell looked like a slightly curved tray. Friday rubbed the inside of it with sand.

"It's a shield," he explained to Robinson. "It can't be pierced by an arrow and even a *bola* just bounces off them."

Robinson was very angry with Friday for his cruelty to the turtle. But a few days later he saw how kind and gentle he could be to an animal he had adopted.

Unfortunately, his latest friend was a baby vulture abandoned by its parents—a dreadful little beast with bulging eyes, great clumsy feet and a scrawny naked body. When anyone came near it it opened its enormous beak and squealed.

First Friday gave the little vulture scraps of fresh meat which it gobbled up. Soon the little bird showed signs of illness; it slept all the day, its crop sticking out like a hard ball. It was because of the meat, which had been too fresh and had given it indigestion. So Friday placed the entrails of a goat out in the sun to rot. They were soon crawling with fat white worms which Friday collected in a shell. He then put the worms in his mouth and chewed them very slowly.

[61]

In the end he had produced a thick white mash which he fed to the baby vulture.

The sight made Robinson a bit ill, and he escaped into the house. All the same he couldn't help admiring Friday for all the trouble he had taken to help the poor creature.

CHAPTER NINE

Since Friday had arrived on the island Robinson hadn't gone back to his hole in the cave. He hoped that now that he had company, life on the island with all its work and official duties would keep him happy and that he would have no need of such drugs.

But one night when the moon was full he woke up and couldn't get back to sleep. There wasn't a breath of wind outside. The trees were so still they seemed to be asleep— just like Friday and Tenn, who as usual were curled up together outside the door. At night there was no work he could possibly do. He had no reason to put on his uniform, no reason to be a governor or a general. It was like a vacation. Robinson wished the night would go on forever, but he knew that the day would come again with all its worries and obligations. So he got up, opened the door, stepped over Friday and Tenn, and headed for the cave where the night and its dreams never ended.

The next morning Friday was very much surprised at

Robinson's absence. He had slept two hours more than usual because Robinson hadn't come to wake him, and he felt very cheerful. What should he do? Of course, there were the cabbages to water and the goats to milk, and there was work to be done on the little observation post at the top of the great cedar. But with Robinson gone all these white man's obligations were forgotten and Friday was an Indian again. He looked around and his eyes fell on the big chest that Robinson kept under his bed. He knew what was in it, and suddenly he had an idea. He dragged the chest over the floor, and once outside the house hoisted it on his shoulder. Then he set out, followed by Tenn.

In the northwestern part of the island there was a meadow tucked away in the dunes. At one end of it was a clump of cactus. These plants had the strangest shapes. They looked like a procession of green rubber dolls covered with knobs and bristles. Some had tails, some had trunks and others seemed to be carrying tennis racquets.

By the time he reached the meadow Friday's shoulder was sore. He dropped the chest on the ground; the hinges snapped and the lid flew open. The contents—magnificent garments and precious jewels—fell out every which way. Friday would never have thought of arraying himself in such finery. But what fun it would be to dress up the cactuses, which looked something like human beings and were just the right size. He spent over an hour putting breeches on the gentlemen and dresses on the ladies. He added hats, capes, shawls, gloves, and then went round distributing

bracelets, earrings and diadems. At the bottom of the chest he found parasols, lorgnettes and fans which he arranged cleverly in their hands. Then he paused to look at his work, at this fantastic assembly of lords and ladies who seemed to be bowing to one another as if performing a dance. Friday laughed and leapt about imitating them, while Tenn romped and barked for joy. Then Friday turned his back on the spectacle and headed for the beach.

It was a perfect day and Friday sang for joy as he ran naked over the pure white sand. How beautiful he was, alone with the sun and his dog, happy, free to do whatever he liked, far from that tedious Robinson! He gathered shells, lavender, blue or mottled, so much prettier in their simplicity than the big complicated jewels he had decorated the cactuses with. He threw pebbles down the beach and Tenn ran after them barking and brought them back. Then he threw pieces of wood into the water and the dog swam after them, churning the water with his four paws. When he turned around with a stick in his mouth, the waves carried him back to the shore.

In the course of their wanderings they came to the rice paddy which glittered in the sun like a mirror. Friday picked up a flat stone and skipped it over the water. It skipped seven times and sank without a splash. But then something happened that Friday hadn't expected. Tenn ran after the stone. His momentum carried him about fifty feet, but there he stopped. The water wasn't deep enough for him to swim in, and he sank into the mud. He turned and tried to come back. Once he managed to jump clear of the mud but he fell back and thrashed about frantically. Friday took a few steps toward the dangerous muddy water. He was about to jump in and save Tenn, but then he had a better idea. He ran to the sluice that served to drain the paddy and tugged at the gate with all his might. There was a frothing and bubbling outside the gate while inside the water level quickly dropped. In a few minutes all the water was gone from the paddy. The rice crop would be ruined but at least Tenn was able to crawl out through the mud.

Friday danced off to the woods, leaving Tenn behind to roll in the sand and clean himself up.

Robinson spent thirty-six hours in the cave. When he finally came home there was no sign of Friday. Only Tenn was waiting faithfully at the door. He had an uneasy, guilty look, and it was he who led Robinson first to the cactuses covered with fine clothes and jewels and then to the rice paddy, where the year's crop lay parched in the sun. Robinson flew into a terrible rage. He closed the drainage sluice and opened the feed sluice on the off chance that the plants might recover. Then he spent several hours picking the clothes and jewelry, his most precious possessions, off the cactuses, pricking his fingers cruelly in the process. The worst of it was that he felt guilty: if he hadn't gone down into the cave, all this wouldn't have happened. And that made him even more furious.

The next day he went looking for Friday. His anger had died down and he was beginning to be worried. With Tenn's help he searched the forest. The dog seemed to understand that it was up to him to find Friday. He slipped into clumps of bushes and thickets. Now and then he picked up Friday's scent, followed it for a while and lost it. Then at last, in a small clearing, he found what must have been Friday's secret camp. He had slung a hammock of lianas between two trees and padded it with dry grass. It looked *very* comfortable. Nearby a plaited straw doll with a wooden head and raffia hair was sitting in a chair made of interlaced branches. Friday had made himself a little friend for company. Robinson saw strewn about all sorts of things that Friday had made to amuse himself with: a reed flute, a blowpipe, darts, feather headdresses like those worn by the North American Indians, a little guitar, and so on. Robinson was amazed and also a little jealous to see how well Friday seemed to get along without him. If the life of a savage could be so amusing what was the use of all his work and all the duties he set himself?

Friday couldn't be far away. Suddenly Tenn stopped at the edge of a clump of magnolia overgrown with ivy, and pointed. Then he inched forward with pricked-up ears and tensed muscles. Finally he stopped again and laid his muzzle close to the trunk of a tree. The branches stirred and Friday's laughter rang out. He had hidden his head under a helmet of leaves and flowers. With the juice of the *genipap* —the stems of which yield a green dye when crushed—he had painted leaves and branches all over his body. Thus disguised as a plant and still laughing merrily, he danced in triumph around Robinson, then away he ran to the sea to wash in the waves.

CHAPTER TEN

The daily routine started in again. Robinson kept pretending to be the governor and commanding general of the island. Friday pretended to work hard in the interest of civilization. Tenn didn't pretend anything, he just napped all day. He was growing fat and sluggish in his old age.

Friday discovered a new pastime. He found the hiding place where Robinson kept Captain Van Deyssel's tobacco jar and china-bowl pipe. Whenever he had a chance, he went to the cave and smoked. If Robinson found out, he would be sure to punish him severely because there was very little tobacco left and he himself had taken to smoking only on special occasions.

One day Robinson went down to the beach to inspect the fishing lines which lay bare at low tide. Friday tucked the tobacco jar under his arm and went to the cave. He had made himself a kind of easy chair out of sacks and barrels. He leaned back and drew deeply on the pipe. Then he blew the smoke out and watched the bluish cloud spread in the dim light. He was about to take another puff when he heard shouts and barking in the distance. Robinson had come home sooner than he expected and was calling him in an angry voice. Tenn was yapping. A few moments later Friday heard the snapping of Robinson's whip. He must have noticed that the tobacco jar was gone. Friday stood up. Oh well, he'd just go out and take his punishment. Suddenly he stopped still: what was he to do with the pipe that he was holding in his hand? He threw it with all his might deep into the back of the cave where the kegs of powder were stored.

Then he went bravely to meet Robinson, who of course was furious. At the sight of Friday, he raised the whip. At that moment the forty kegs of powder exploded and a torrent of red flame flew out from the cave. Robinson felt himself lifted into the air as he watched the great boulders of the cave come tumbling down like a child's building blocks.

The first thing Robinson saw when he opened his eyes was a dark face leaning over him. Friday was holding up Robinson's head with one hand and was trying to make him drink some water which he held in the hollow of the other hand. But Robinson's teeth were clenched and the water ran down over his beard and chest.

When Friday saw Robinson move, he smiled and stood up. A part of his shirt and his left trouser leg were torn and blackened. When he moved, they fell to the ground. He burst out laughing and wriggled out of the rest of his clothes. In a pile of broken household articles he found a piece of a mirror, looked into it, made faces at himself, and with another burst of laughter handed it to Robinson. Robinson wasn't seriously hurt but he was black with soot and his beautiful red beard was half burned away. Standing up, he too shook off his charred rags. He took a few steps. He was covered with soot and dirt but he had only a few bruises.

The house was burning like a torch. The wall of the fortress had collapsed into the moat. All the other buildings, the church, the bank and the stables had been blasted into a heap of rubble. The calendar must have disappeared. As the two of them surveyed the devastation a column of earth rose into the air a hundred feet away; then half a second later a terrible explosion hurled them both to the ground. It was the charge of powder which Robinson had buried at the edge of the woods, equipped with a long fuse that he would have been able to light from inside the fort.

Terrified by this second explosion much closer to them than the first, the goats had stampeded and broken down the fence of their enclosure. Now they were galloping off in all directions. They would scatter all over the island and soon be wild again.

The mouth of the cave was blocked by a pile of rocks. One rock rose like a steeple over the confusion. Robinson looked around him and mechanically picked up various objects which the cave must have spat out before the rocks fell. There was a musket with a twisted barrel, some torn sacks and crushed baskets. Friday did the same, but instead of piling up the things he had found at the foot of the cedar as Robinson was doing, he finished destroying them. Robinson did not interfere, but his heart sank when he saw Friday picking up handfuls of wheat he had found in a tub and scattering them to the wind.

Night was falling. They had just found something that was not broken—the spyglass—when at the foot of the tree they came across Tenn's body. Friday felt him all over, looking for signs of life. There seemed to be no broken bones and he wasn't wounded. Poor Tenn, so old, so faithful. Perhaps the explosion had caused him to die of fright.

The wind rose. They went down to the beach together and bathed. They shared a bunch of wild bananas and Robinson remembered that a banana was the first thing he had had to eat on the island after the shipwreck. Then they lay down under the big cedar and tried to sleep.

Robinson looked at the moon between the black branches and thought. All the work he had done on the island, his tilled fields, his crops, his provisions, all the houses he had built were lost. Though Friday was the cause of it all, Robinson wasn't angry. To tell the truth, he had long been bored with all the civilization he had built up, but hadn't had the courage to destroy it. Now they were free. Robinson wondered what their life would be like, and he realized that from then on Friday would be the leader.

He was still looking at the sky and thinking when suddenly he saw the moon slip behind a branch and reappear on the other side of it. It seemed to stop there for a moment before slipping off into the night sky. At that moment a terrible creaking and cracking were heard. Robinson and Friday jumped to their feet. It wasn't the moon that had moved, but the tree! The explosion had shaken its roots and now it was reeling in the night wind. A moment later the great cedar fell, crushing dozens of smaller trees and causing the earth to tremble.

CHAPTER ELEVEN

Friday started the new life by taking long, long naps. He spent whole days in the hammock of plaited lianas he had slung between two palm trees not far from the beach. He lay so still that birds would light on the bushes surrounding him. Then, without stirring from his hammock, he would reach for his blowpipe, and in the evening he and Robinson would roast the birds he had bagged in this leisurely way.

Robinson changed completely. Before the explosion his long beard had made him look like a grandfather, but he had kept his hair clipped short. Now he cut his beard, which was already badly singed, and let his hair grow. The effect was to make him look much younger, not at all like a governor, let alone a general.

His body changed too. Because of his fair skin he had always been afraid of sunburn. When he was obliged to work in the sun, he had covered himself from top to toe and worn a hat, while Friday held the broad goatskin sunshade over his head. His skin had been as white and tender as the skin of a plucked chicken.

Friday persuaded him to expose himself to the sun. At first he felt ashamed and sat huddled in the sand. But in a little while he blossomed out. His skin hardened and took on a copper-colored tan, and he grew proud of his rippling muscles and strong chest. He and Friday played games and had contests; they swam, they raced along the beach, they performed high-jumps, they threw the *bola*. Robinson even learned to walk on his hands!

Most of all he watched Friday, and the more he watched the more he learned how to live on a desert island.

Friday spent a great deal of time making bows and arrows. First he carved a plain bow out of the most flexible wood he could find—hazel, sandalwood, amaranth or copaiba. Then he would reinforce the bow by binding strips of goat's horn to it, which made it much more powerful and durable.

Making the arrows was the hardest work. He needed a powerful bow because he liked to make his arrows as long as possible. Some of them measured over five feet in length. An arrow has three parts: the tip, the shaft and the feathering. These three parts must be perfectly balanced. Friday tested his arrows by balancing them on the sharp edge of a rock. For the feathering he used bird feathers when they were available, or palm leaves. He didn't make the tips of stone or metal, but of bone; very often he chipped the bone from the shoulder blade of a goat. Robinson soon realized that Friday did not make these long, strong precise arrows merely to hunt birds and rabbits with. He wanted his arrows to fly high in the sky and to stay there as long as possible. He made arrows mainly for the pleasure of seeing them glide through the sky like gulls.

One day when the sea wind was blowing up whitecaps, Robinson saw Friday shooting arrows straight at the sun. He chose a very long one, over six feet in length. Its albatross feathering measured at least eighteen inches. He drew the bow with all his strength, aiming in the direction of the forest, at an angle of forty-five degrees. The bowstring shot forward, slapping the leather band he wore on his forearm to protect it. The arrow rose about one hundred feet. Then it seemed to hesitate and instead of diving, it leveled off and was carried away by the wind. When it had disappeared behind the trees, Friday turned to Robinson with a broad smile.

"It will fall in the branches," said Robinson. "You'll never find it."

"No, I'll never find it," replied Friday. "But that's because it will never fall."

Before the explosion Robinson had made Friday do the kind of cooking he had learned at home in York. At the beginning of his stay on the island, he had been obliged to roast his meat over the fire, but as soon as he had the necessary equipment he had taken to boiling it—the most usual way of cooking meat in England in those days. But now Friday taught him the Araucanian

way of preparing food and some other recipes that he had made up.

Friday liked to eat as well as possible, but the main thing was to eat when and where he pleased and not to be bothered with a kitchen or cooking utensils. All the pots and dishes had been destroyed by the explosion. When they ate any kind of fowl, Friday usually prepared it in clay. That was the simplest and most amusing way.

He cleaned the fowl and seasoned the inside with salt, pepper and aromatic herbs. Sometimes he stuffed it. He left all the feathers on. Then he prepared moist clay—not too wet, just moist enough to knead. He kneaded the clay into the shape of a large pancake about half an inch thick. Then he folded it around the bird and pressed the edges together carefully. In the end he had something that looked rather like a clay football. Next he dug a hole in the ground and made a wood fire in it. When the fire had burned down a little, he laid the clay ball on the coals and added more wood from time to time to keep up the fire for an hour or two The clay dried like a piece of pottery. When it was very hard, he took it out of the hole and broke it open. The feathers came off with the clay and the fowl was as tender and tasty as if it had been baked in an oven. What Friday liked best about this way of cooking was that you smashed your cooking pot every time; there were no dishes to wash or put away.

Robinson had been in the habit of boiling his eggs, but Friday taught him how to manage without any pot or water.

By twisting a wire he had made a kind of egg cradle, which he held over the fire.

Robinson had always thought that a good cook should never mix meat and fish, or salt and sugar. Friday showed him that such mixtures could be delicious. Before roasting a slice of peccary, he cut deep slits in the meat and filled them with raw oysters or mussels. Robinson had to admit that the dish was excellent.

Friday had several ways of mixing the sweet with the salty; for instance, he would wrap a fish in slices of pineapple before cooking it, or stuff a rabbit with plums. He also taught Robinson how to make sugar. He would chop down a certain kind of palm tree which is shaped like a ninepin, that is, thicker in the middle than at the base or the top. Then he would strip the leaves and cut off the upper end. Drops of thick, sweet sap began to ooze from this cut. Sap always rises in a tree trunk and liquid sugar kept on flowing for months, though from time to time Friday had to slice off a little more wood so that the pores of the tree did not get clogged.

Friday showed Robinson how to make caramel by exposing the sugary syrup to fire. He coated fruits with this caramel before toasting them. And he also used the syrup in cooking meat and fish.

CHAPTER TWELVE

It was over a question of food that Robinson and Friday had their first quarrel. Before the explosion, a quarrel between them had been unthinkable. Robinson was the master and Friday simply had to obey. Robinson could scold Friday or even beat him. But now Friday was free. He was Robinson's equal.

Friday had put chunks of snake meat topped with grasshoppers into a large seashell. He had been getting on Robinson's nerves for several days. Such irritation is a very bad thing when two people are condemned to live by themselves on a desert island. The day before Robinson had had indigestion, brought on by turtle steak topped with blueberries. And now Friday was about to serve up this snake and insect stew. Overcome with disgust, Robinson kicked the big shell and sent the contents rolling into the sand. Friday was furious. He picked up the shell in both hands and brandished it over Robinson's head.

Were the two friends going to fight? No. Friday ran away. Two hours later he reappeared, dragging a kind of dummy after him. Its head was made of a coconut, its legs and arms of bamboo stalks. It was dressed in Robinson's old clothes and looked like a scarecrow. A naval officer's cap was perched on the head, and the face, drawn by Friday, was Robinson's own! He stood the dummy on its feet.

"Permit me," he said, "to introduce Robinson Crusoe, Governor of the Island of Speranza."

Then he picked up the empty shell that Robinson had kicked, and with a roar smashed it against the coconut. The bamboo limbs broke under the blow and the whole dummy collapsed. Then Friday burst out laughing and threw his arms around Robinson.

Robinson understood the lesson. One day when Friday was eating fat palm worms rolled in ants' eggs, Robinson went off to the beach in disgust. In the wet sand he modeled a statue lying on its belly, its head and hair made of seaweed. The face was hidden in the crook of one arm, but the brown body certainly bore a resemblance to Friday. Robinson had just finished his work when Friday appeared, his mouth full of palm worms.

"Permit me," said Robinson, "to introduce Friday, the man who eats snakes and worms."

Then he broke off a hazel branch and started beating the sand-Friday, for that was what he had made him for.

After that there were four of them on the island, the real Robinson and the dummy Robinson, the real Friday and the sand-Friday. And all the wicked things the two friends might have done to each other they did to the two copies.

They beat or insulted them, but to each other they were always polite and friendly.

One afternoon when Robinson was taking a nap under a eucalyptus tree, Friday woke him rather roughly. He had disguised himself. Around his legs he had wrapped rags that resembled trousers and over his shoulders he had slipped a short jacket. He wore a straw hat and as if that weren't sufficient protection from the sun, he carried a large sunshade made of palm fronds. The most striking thing about the disguise was the false beard he had achieved by sticking wads of cotton on his cheeks.

He strode majestically up to Robinson and asked: "Do you know who I am?"

"No."

"I am Robinson Crusoe of York, master of the savage Friday."

"Then who am I?" Robinson asked.

"Guess . . ."

Robinson knew Friday too well not to be able to figure out what the answer was. He got up and disappeared into the woods.

If Friday was Robinson, the Robinson of old, master of the slave Friday, then Robinson must transform himself into Friday, the Friday of old, the slave of Robinson. Actually, now that his hair had grown and he no longer had his beard, he looked so much like Friday that he had very little to do. He merely rubbed his face and body with nut juice and put on the leather apron that Friday had been wearing the day he appeared on the island. Then he came back and said:

"There! Now I am Friday."

Friday spoke in long sentences using his best English, and Robinson answered with the few words of Araucan he had learned in the days when Friday knew no English at all.

"I have saved you," said Friday, "from your fellow Indians who wanted to sacrifice you to the evil powers."

And Robinson knelt and bowed his head to the ground, stammering words of thanks. Then he took Friday's foot and placed it on his own neck.

They often played that game. It was always Friday who began it. The moment he appeared with his sunshade and false beard, Robinson understood and began to play the part of Friday. They never invented anything new but always played true scenes from their past life, scenes from the days when Friday was a terrified slave and Robinson a severe master. They acted out the story of the cactuses dressed in their finery, they acted out the story of the drained-out rice paddy, and the story of the pipe smoked in secret only a few steps from the stores of gunpowder. But the scene Friday liked to act out the best was the first one, the one in which Robinson saved him from the Indians who wanted to kill him.

Robinson understood that Friday liked this game because it enabled him to come to terms with his past life as a slave.

And Robinson was happy to play it because he felt sorry he had been a hard master to Friday and his conscience still troubled him.

One day Friday went out for a walk and came back with a keg over his shoulder. He had found it while chasing a lizard in the sand near the old fort.

Robinson thought for a while and then remembered how he had buried two kegs of powder and connected them with the fort by a fuse. Only one had been blown up after the explosion. And now Friday had found the other. Robinson was surprised to see him so happy about it.

"What can we do with it?" he asked. "You know we haven't got a gun."

Friday didn't answer. He merely pried open the lid with his knife. Then he took a handful of powder and threw it into the fire. Robinson jumped back, expecting an explosion. But there was no explosion; instead, a tall green flame flared up, then vanished.

"You see," Friday explained. "A gun is the worst way of burning gunpowder. When it's shut up in the gun, the powder gets angry, and when you let it out it makes a big noise. If you leave it alone and free, it's quiet and beautiful."

He asked Robinson to throw a handful into the fire, and when the flame shot up, Friday sprang to his feet as though to dance with it. Again and again they threw handfuls of the powder into the flame. Great green curtains of flame rose in the air, and each time Friday did a different dance.

Later on they thought of another way of playing with the gunpowder. They gathered pine gum—which burns very nicely all by itself—and mixed it with powder in a bowl. In this way they obtained a sticky paste which they smeared on the trunk and branches of a dead tree near the cliff. That night they set it on fire. The whole tree sparkled like a golden chandelier and went on burning until morning.

They worked for several days making fire-paste out of the powder that was left and coating all the dead trees on the island with it. At night if they were bored and couldn't sleep, they would set fire to the tree and turn the night into a festival.

CHAPTER THIRTEEN

The goats that Robinson had domesticated and shut up in pens had by now become completely wild. But, like almost all animals that live in freedom, they had banded together in herds commanded by the strongest and wisest males. The ruler of them all was Andoar, the largest and strongest he-goat on the island.

When danger threatened a herd, they would all gather together on a hill or rocky crag. The males formed a ring around the kids and females, and lowered their heads, confronting the enemy with a menacing row of horns.

Friday thought up a dangerous game. When he met a he-goat alone, he would wrestle with him. If the goat ran away, Friday would run after him, seize him by the horns and wrestle him to the ground. When he had defeated the goat he would mark him by fitting a collar of lianas around his neck.

Once when he was out chasing a he-goat, Friday found a wounded kid in the hollow of some rocks. It was a female, all white and very young, still without horns. She had a fractured foreleg. Friday whittled splints from two sticks and attached them to the fractured bone. An older and more reasonable animal might have put up with this contraption, but Anda—for that was the name Friday gave the kid— refused to lie still. She jumped wildly about and hurt herself even more by falling on the splints. In the end she managed to throw them off and toppled over on her side whimpering pathetically.

Because she suffered so dreadfully Robinson thought they would have to kill her. It is true that in most parts of the world four-legged beasts that have broken a limb are done away with because they cannot bear to be imprisoned in splints or plaster. But Friday insisted on saving Anda. He kept her still by making a heavy wooden frame and tying her to it in such a way that she had to lie on her side. Of course she bleated pathetically at first, but in the end she resigned herself and accepted the fragrant grass and fresh water that Friday brought her twice a day.

After three weeks Friday set Anda free. She was eager to run about and leap, but her muscles had grown stiff and she staggered about as if she had been drinking. Friday had to teach her how to walk again. He was very patient. Taking her between his legs and holding her by the sides he walked slowly step by step while the little kid's hooves teetered and stumbled in the grass. In the end she was able to leap and gallop again, and it was a joy to see her bounding from rock to rock, sometimes behind Friday, sometimes ahead of him. Soon he had a hard time keeping up with her.

But even after she had learned to run again, Anda never wanted to graze by herself. Friday could put her in the middle of a meadow full of grass and flowers, or under a young tree covered with leaves—goats prefer leaves to grass—and she would bleat for Friday until he came and fed her the leaves or grass he had picked for her.

They were inseparable. At night she curled up with him and kept him warm. In the daytime she never stirred from his side.

"And you know," he said to Robinson. "Later on, when she has milk, I won't milk her the way we used to milk our goats. Oh no. Her milk will be all for me, and I'll drink it straight from her udders."

He laughed with joy at the idea. Robinson couldn't help feeling a little jealous; he felt left out of their friendship.

"Ever since the explosion," he said, "you've wanted everybody on Speranza to be free. No more domestic animals, you said. Then why do you keep Anda with you all the time?"

"Anda isn't a domestic animal," said Friday with great dignity. "She stays with me because she loves me. The day she wants to leave, I won't stop her."

One morning Friday woke up with the feeling that something had happened while he was asleep. Anda was lying there as usual, but something about her seemed to have changed. And there was a strange, strong smell in the air. He didn't say anything but he thought about it all day.

The next night Friday only shut half an eye. At midnight

the bush beside which he was lying seemed to open like an enormous flower and protruding from it was the most beautiful goat's head he had ever seen. It had long gleaming eyes, a fine silky beard, and gigantic black, ringed horns. There was a terrible smell of goat hair and musk. Friday recognized Andoar, king of the goats of Speranza. Anda must have seen him too for she stirred gently, as though trying to slip away without waking him. But Friday kept a strong grip on her until the big he-goat had left. Then he remembered what he had said to Robinson: that if Anda wanted to leave, he wouldn't stop her. And he blushed with shame under his brown skin.

The next day he gathered brightly colored lianas and plaited a collar that was stronger and more beautiful than any he had made before. The collar was for King Andoar, and Friday started up the mountain in search of him.

He saw him standing on a rock, as motionless as a great hairy statue. He climbed up slowly, holding in his teeth the fine collar that would mark his victory over Andoar. At the top of the rock there was hardly enough room for both of them. The goat didn't stir a muscle. Friday wondered what to do. Should he make the first move? He came closer, holding the collar at arm's length. He was about to reach out and touch Andoar when the animal lunged forward, imprisoning Friday's waist between his horns. Then the goat jerked his head to one side and Friday lost his balance and fell off the rock. Luckily the rock wasn't very high, but Friday landed in a clump of holly and thorn bushes and his skin was badly torn.

For several days he had to lie in his hammock. Robinson made him compresses of wet moss and Anda licked his wounds. Friday kept talking about Andoar. He had made up his mind to meet him again and get even, but being a good sport he had nothing but praise for the king of the goats. Andoar's presence, he said, could be detected a hundred paces off, just by the horrible smell. Andoar never ran away. Andoar hadn't tried to kill him after his fall from the rock, as any other he-goat would have done.

Friday was very weak. He left his hammock only to gather grass and draw water for Anda. One night he fell into a deep sleep. When he awoke very late next morning, Anda was gone. "You see," he said to Robinson. "She wanted to leave and she left."

After that Friday was more determined than ever to find Andoar and put the collar of lianas on him. Then he would bring Anda back.

When Friday was well again, Robinson tried to persuade him not to wrestle with the king of the goats. This was a very dangerous game. What if that rock had been higher? But his entreaties fell on deaf ears. Friday wanted his revenge and he didn't care about the risk. One morning he set out for the big rocks in search of his enemy.

He didn't have to look very long. In the distance he saw the great he-goat surrounded by kids and females who fled wildly at Friday's approach. Only one little white kid remained faithfully beside the king, and Friday couldn't help recognizing Anda. She wasn't grazing; Andoar was grazing for her. He tore off a tuft of grass and brought it to her.

[91]

Anda bit into it and nodded her head several times as though to say thank you. Friday felt a pang of jealousy.

Andoar didn't try to run away. He was standing on a kind of platform with a steep cliff on one side and a precipice on the other.

Friday had twined the collar around his waist. He unrolled it and challenged Andoar by shaking it under his nose. The goat stopped chewing but still held a long blade of grass between his teeth. Then he grinned into his beard, stood up on his hind legs, and took a few steps toward Friday, brandishing his forepaws in the air, and nodding his enormous horns as though waving to a crowd of admirers. Friday was so amazed at the goat's antics that he forgot the danger. The beast was only a few steps away. Suddenly he dropped his forelegs to the ground and lunged at Friday. Friday jumped to one side, but he was just a second too late. A violent blow in the shoulder spun him around and he fell on the rocks.

If he had gotten up right away, Andoar would have attacked him again, so he lay flat on his back. Between his half-closed lids he saw nothing but a patch of blue sky. Suddenly the sky darkened. A little beard and a shaggy head were leaning over him. The muzzle was twisted in a kind of grin. Friday tried to move but a terrible pain shot through his shoulder and he fainted.

When he opened his eyes the sun was directly overhead and the heat was unbearable. He propped himself up on his left hand. The cliff reflected the light like a mirror. No sign of the goat. Friday staggered to his feet and was about to turn around when he heard hoofbeats on the rocks behind him. They were coming so fast that he couldn't get into a fighting position, so he threw himself on the ground. A blow in the hip sent him reeling. Andoar had stopped short and was standing beside him. Friday lost his balance completely and fell on the goat's back. Andoar almost collapsed under the weight, then righted himself and set off at a gallop.

In agony from the pain in his shoulder, Friday clung to the beast. His hands gripped the base of the horns, his legs squeezed Andoar's flanks, and he dug his toes into the wool. Andoar made fantastic leaps to throw him off. He ran round and round the rocky platform, never once losing his foothold. Friday was in such pain that he was afraid of fainting again. He had to do something to make Andoar stop. He ran his hands down over the animal's head until they covered his eyes. If he were blinded, Friday thought, he would have to stop. But Andoar did not stop. He ran straight ahead, for he could no longer see the obstacles in his path. His hoofs clattering over the rocks, he ran blindly to the precipice and, still locked together, the two bodies fell.

From two miles away Robinson had watched the struggle through his spyglass and seen the two contestants fall. He was familiar enough with that part of the island to know that he could reach the bottom

of the ravine by a little path that twined along the side of the mountain.

Night was falling when he found Andoar's body in a sparse clump of bushes. Holding his nose, he bent down over the big brown body and saw the colored collar knotted tightly around his neck. Hearing laughter behind him, he stood up, turned around and saw Friday standing there. He was cruelly scratched and his shoulder was out of joint, but he seemed perfectly happy. Anda stood beside him, licking his hand.

"He was under me," he explained. "That's what saved me. The king of goats died saving me, but I'll make him fly and sing."

CHAPTER FOURTEEN

Robinson was amazed at the speed of Friday's recovery. A few days later, Friday went back to Andoar's body. First he cut off the head and put it in the middle of an anthill. Then he cut the skin above the hoofs and the whole length of the chest and belly. After that the body slipped easily out of the fleece. Of the body he saved only the intestines, which he washed well and hung over the branches of a tree to dry. He threw the heavy, greasy fleece over his shoulder and, singing merrily, took it down to the beach. He let the waves roll over it until it was impregnated with salt and sand, and and then scraped it with a shell. This work took several days. When he had finished, he stretched the hide over a frame like a drumskin. When it was dry, he polished it with pumice stone.

He still refused to tell Robinson what he was doing. But he kept shouting gleefully: "Andoar's going to fly. Andoar's going to fly."

Since his earliest childhood Robinson had been given to dizziness. Even to climb up on a chair had made his head spin. One day his father had taken him to visit the belfry of the cathedral in York. They had climbed the steep, dimly-lit winding stairs, and then suddenly Robinson had found himself out in the open, looking down on the whole city and its people, who were no bigger than ants. He had howled for fright, and his father had had to throw his jacket over his head and carry him down the stairs like a bundle.

For some time now he had been forcing himself to climb a tree every morning to cure himself of his dizziness. In the past he would have thought such an exercise useless and ridiculous. But now that he had taken Friday as his model, it seemed very important.

That morning he decided to climb an araucaria, one of the biggest trees on the island. He took hold of the lowest branch and hoisted himself up on one knee. Then he swung himself from branch to branch, thinking that he would see the sun rise a little earlier than usual if he got to the top. The higher he climbed the more the tree trembled and swayed in the wind. And the more the tree trembled and swayed the dizzier he became. Not far from the top he made a mistake that is hard to avoid when you are worried about dizziness: he looked down. All he could see was a jumble of branches that seemed to be spinning. Paralyzed by fear, he clutched the trunk in his arms and legs. Then finally he realized that he must look *up* and not *down*. He raised his eyes. In the blue sky a great, golden, diamond-shaped bird was floating in the wind. Friday had kept his mysterious promise: he had made Andoar fly.

He had tied three lengths of reed together crosswise. At the ends he had cut grooves and had strung gut between them. On this light but strong frame he had placed Andoar's skin, folding over the edges and sewing them to the gut. The two ends of the longest reed were joined by a slack cord to which the kite string was attached at a point carefully calculated so that the kite would ride at the proper angle.

Friday had been working on his kite since the crack of dawn. When it was finished, he picked it up and it had flapped and quivered in the wind as though impatient to take flight. Friday then took it to the beach and shouted for joy as Andoar, bent like a bow, had sped into the air like a rocket, dragging behind him a tail of white and black feathers.

Robinson hurried down from his tree to join Friday. He was lying on his back in the sand, his head cradled in his arms, the kite string attached to one of his ankles. Anda was curled up in a ball at his feet. Robinson lay down beside him and for a long time they watched Andoar flying fitfully through the clouds, rising and falling, vibrating in a sudden gust of wind and taking a deep plunge when the wind slackened. Suddenly Friday jumped to his feet and, with the kite string still attached to his ankle, began to imitate Andoar's sky dance. Laughing and singing, he leapt into the air with arms outstretched. He landed on his toes, knelt down, leapt up again, flung out his left leg and spun about. All the while Anda gambolled about him. And high in the clouds the golden bird, attached to Friday's ankle by a thousand feet of string, danced along with him, leapt, plunged, wheeled and leapt again.

That afternoon they went kite fishing, as the Solomon Islanders do. The kite string was fastened to the stern of the canoe. Another string of the same length connected the tail of the kite with a hook hidden under a tuft of feathers. Robinson paddled slowly against the wind; far behind the canoe the tuft of feathers danced over the crests of the waves. Now and then a fish snapped at the feathers and its jaws closed on the hook. Then the kite would bob like a float and the fishermen knew they had a fish on the line. Robinson would turn around and, since he was now paddling with the wind, quickly reach the hook. Friday would haul the fish in. It was usually a belone, long and glistening, with a green back and glistening silver sides.

Friday didn't want to bring Andoar down for the night. He tied him to one of the pepper trees from which his hammock was slung, and that was how it was that Andoar, like a domestic animal on its tether, passed the night near his master. The next day Andoar followed Friday wherever he went. But during the second night the wind died down and in the morning Friday found him lying in a flowering meadow. He tried to send him into the sky again but gave up after several unsuccessful attempts. After that Friday seemed to forget Andoar and for a whole week he did little else than sleep. Then he remembered the goat's head which he had left on an anthill.

The ants had done their work well. Nothing was left of the flesh or of the long brown and white hair. Even the inside of the head had been cleaned out. When Friday joined Robinson that evening he was holding up a beautiful white skull, which with its two magnificent curved horns had the shape of a lyre. He had decorated the horns with Andoar's collar of lianas.

"Andoar is going to sing," he announced mysteriously.

First he whittled two sticks of unequal length out of sycamore wood. At the ends of the longer one he drilled holes into which he inserted the tips of the horns. The shorter stick was fastened parallel to the first, halfway down the horn. A little higher up, between the eye sockets, he placed a bridge of pine wood with twelve narrow grooves at its upper edge. Andoar's intestines were still hanging on a tree, but by now the sun had reduced them to thin, dry ribbons. Friday took them down and cut them into strips about a yard long.

When Robinson saw him fasten the strips of gut to the cross pieces with pegs, he knew that Friday was making an aeolian harp, an instrument played by the wind as it blows through the strings. The strings must be tuned in unison or in octaves because, when the wind is blowing exactly right, they all sound at once.

To each side of the skull Friday attached the wing of a vulture to turn the strings into the wind. Then he put the

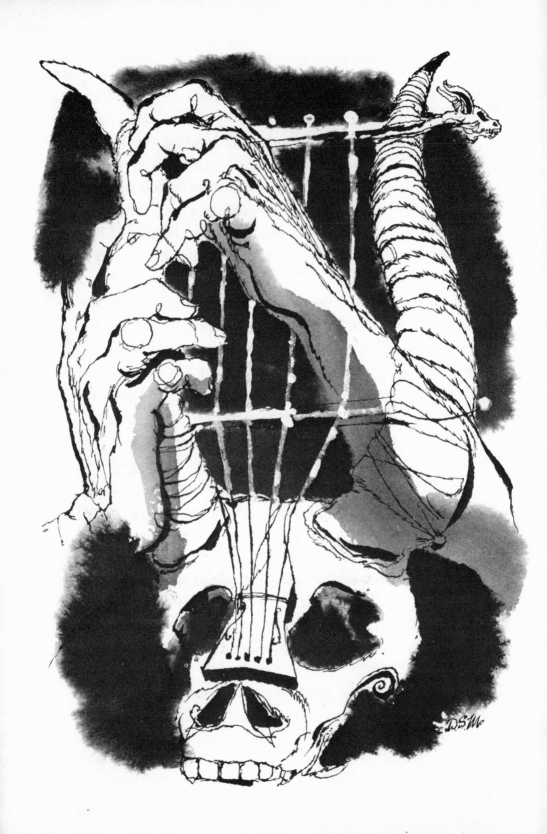

harp in the branches of a dead cypress tree. Instantly a thin, plaintive sigh was heard, though the air seemed perfectly still. For a long while Friday listened to the soft, sad music. Then he made a scornful face and turned to Robinson, raising two fingers, meaning that there wasn't enough wind and that only two strings were sounding. They had to wait a whole month before Andoar consented to sing with his full voice.

Robinson had finally set up housekeeping in the branches of an araucaria, where he had built a shelter out of slabs of bark. One night Friday climbed up and pulled him by the toes. A storm had come up and the moon could be seen racing in and out of the tattered clouds. Friday led Robinson to the cypress. Even before the tree came in sight, Robinson seemed to hear a heavenly orchestra of flutes and violins. By the time the two friends reached the foot of the singing tree, the wind had redoubled in violence. Attached by a short string to the highest branch, the kite was throbbing like a drumskin, now motionless, now leaping wildly. In the shifting light of the moon the two vulture's wings opened and closed in response to the wind. The flying Andoar and the singing Andoar were united in a somber festival. And the music was so heartbreakingly sad that it seemed to be the complaint of the king of the goats, who had met his death saving Friday.

Huddled together in the lee of a boulder, Robinson and Friday spent half the night listening to that solemn music that seemed to fall from the stars and rise from the depths of the earth.

CHAPTER FIFTEEN

Friday was picking flowers among the rocks when he saw a little white spot on the eastern horizon. He ran down to tell Robinson, who was shaving. If Robinson was excited by the news, he didn't show it.

"Looks like visitors," he said. "In that case I'll really finish cleaning up."

Friday was excited enough for two. He climbed a tree carrying the spyglass, through which the ship was clearly visible. It was a topsail schooner, built for speed, with two tall masts, one bearing a square sail, the other a triangular one. She was doing ten to twelve knots and was heading for the marshy side of the island. Friday ran down to give this information to Robinson, who was running a big tortoise shell comb through his red mane. Then he climbed back to his observation post. The skipper must have seen that the marshy shore was a poor place for a landing because the ship put about and skirted the coast under shortened sail.

Friday scampered away to tell Robinson that the ship was passing the dunes and would probably anchor in the Bay of Salvation.

The first thing was to find out her nationality. Robinson went to the edge of the trees bordering the beach and looked through the spyglass. The ship was turning into the wind two cable lengths from the shore. A few moments later the jangling of her anchor chain could be heard.

Robinson had never seen that sort of ship before, but she was flying the Union Jack and *that* he recognized. The crew had lowered a boat and it was heading for the shore.

By now Robinson was very excited. He didn't know how long he had been on the island but it seemed to him that he had spent most of his life there. It is said that a man on the point of death sees his whole past spread out before him. And something like that happened to Robinson. He relived everything—the shipwreck, the building of the *Escape* and his failure to launch it, his days of misery in the mudhole, his frantic efforts to civilize the island, the arrival of Friday, his turning of Friday into a slave, the explosion, the destruction of all his work, and then the long years of quiet happiness with Friday. Was all this about to end?

The boat was piled high with casks, it must have been coming ashore for water. In the stern stood a man with a black beard. He had on high boots and was wearing a straw hat; the captain, no doubt. The boat scraped the bottom and came to a stop. The men jumped out into the waves and pulled it up on the beach. The man with the black beard held out his hand to Robinson and introduced himself:

"William Hunter of Blackpool, captain of the schooner *Whitebird*."

"What is the date?" Robinson asked him.

The captain turned in surprise to the man just behind him who must have been the mate.

"What's the date, Joe?"

"Saturday, December 22, 1787, sir."

"Saturday, December 22, 1787," the captain repeated.

Robinson made a quick calculation. The *Virginia* had been wrecked on September 30, 1759. Exactly twenty-eight years, two months and twenty-two days had passed. He couldn't believe he had been on the island so long. In spite of the many things that had happened since he had come to Speranza, it seemed impossible that twenty-eight years could have gone by between the wreck of the *Virginia* and the coming of the *Whitebird*. And another thing: if it was really 1787 as the newcomers said, he must be exactly fifty years old. Fifty! That was the age of an old man. Yet thanks to the free, happy life he had led on Speranza, and thanks most of all to Friday, he was feeling younger every day. He decided, at any rate, not to give the date of his shipwreck for fear of being taken for a liar.

"I was thrown up on this coast by the wreck of the *Virginia*, a galliot commanded by Pieter Van Deyssel of Flushing. I was the sole survivor. Unfortunately, the shock impaired my memory. I've never been able to remember exactly when it happened."

"I've never heard mention of any such ship," said Hunter, "but then we didn't get much news during the war with America."

Naturally Robinson could not have known that the American colonies had declared themselves independent and been at war with England from 1775 to 1782. But he was careful to ask no questions that would have shown up his ignorance.

Meanwhile, Friday helped the men unload the casks and guided them to the nearest spring. Robinson realized that if he was so eager to help the sailors, it was because he hoped to be taken on board the *Whitebird*. He himself was dying to visit this fine ship, so marvelously built for speed and evidently of the most recent design. And yet Captain Hunter, Joseph, the mate, and all these other men struck him as ugly, coarse and brutal, and he wondered if he could ever again get used to living with such people.

Robinson showed the captain around the island, pointing out objects of interest, game birds, fruits and such wild vegetables as water cress and purslane, which not only taste good but also prevent scurvy. Meanwhile the men were climbing the scaly trunks of palm trees and cutting down palm cabbages with their cutlasses; others could be heard laughing as they chased goats. Now and then they caught one and cut its throat on the spot or tied it for future use. It made Robinson miserable to see these drunken brutes mutilating the trees and massacring the animals on his island, but he didn't interfere, for these were the first human beings he had seen in years, and he didn't wish to seem selfish.

On the old site of the Bank of Speranza tall trees were now waving in the wind. Here one of the sailors found two goldpieces. His shouts brought others to the spot. They searched for a while in vain. Then after violent quarrels they decided their chances would be better if they burned the grass. Robinson couldn't help thinking that after all the gold belonged to him and that the goats would now be deprived of the best pasture on the island. Whenever a coin was found, the men fought over it with knives or cutlasses.

Turning away in disgust, Robinson struck up a conversation with the mate. Joseph spoke with enthusiasm of the slave trade. Africans were rounded up, loaded like cattle into special ships, and taken to America, where they were sold to plantation owners. Then the ships took on cotton, sugar, coffee and indigo, which could be sold at a large profit in the ports of Europe. At this point Hunter spoke up and told how he had sunk a French troop transport bringing reinforcements to the American rebels. Every one of those Frenchies had drowned—he still couldn't think of it without laughing. Robinson felt as if he had lifted a stone and uncovered a nest of cockroaches.

The boat made a trip to the *Whitebird* with a load of fruit, vegetables, game, and a few bound and wildly struggling kids. Now the men were waiting for the captain's orders.

"I trust you will do me the honor of dining with me," said the captain to Robinson.

Without waiting for an answer, he ordered the men to take the fresh water to the ship and to come back for him and his guest.

When Robinson stepped onto the deck of the *Whitebird*, he was greeted by a radiant Friday who had come over on the boat's previous trip. The crew had made friends with him, and he seemed to know the ship as well as if he had lived there all his life. Robinson watched him run up the shrouds, hoist himself up into the crow's nest, and continue on over the crosstrees, laughing with glee as he swung through the air fifty feet above the deck. He remembered how Friday loved everything connected with the air—his arrows, his kite, his aeolian harp. And now this graceful white sailing ship with its masts rising skyward. It made Robinson a little sad to see how much happier Friday was than he himself at the arrival of the *Whitebird.*

He had taken a few steps on the deck when he saw a half-naked child tied to the mizzen mast. He looked to be about twelve years old; he was as skinny as a plucked chicken and his back was covered with bleeding welts. He had thick red hair and there were freckles on his scrawny shoulders. Robinson couldn't get a look at his face.

"That's Juan, our cabin boy," the captain explained to Robinson.

And turning to Joseph: "What's he done now?"

A big red face with a cook's hat on it shot out of the galley hatch like a jack-in-the-box.

"I can't do anything with him," said the cook. "This morning he spoiled a chicken pie by salting it three times. I've given him twelve licks of a rope's end, and he'll get more if he doesn't mind what he's doing."

And the head disappeared as quickly as it had popped up.

"Untie him," said the captain. "We'll need him to wait on table."

Robinson dined with the captain and his mate. Friday, he guessed, was eating with the crew. The captain kept piling food on Robinson's plate and Robinson, not wishing to be impolite, forced himself to eat. For years he had eaten only fresh, natural food; he wasn't used to these heavy indigestible dishes.

Half hidden by an enormous white apron, Juan, the cabin boy, waited on table. Robinson tried to catch his eye under his tangled mop of hair, but the boy was so terrified of doing something wrong that he didn't seem to see the guest. The captain was gloomy and silent. Joe kept up the conversation, speaking chiefly of the latest developments in navigation and ship design.

After dinner Hunter retired to his cabin and the mate took Robinson to the captain's bridge. He wanted to show him a new invention, the sextant, which served to measure the height of the sun over the horizon. The instrument was a beautiful piece of workmanship, made of brass, mahogany and ivory. Robinson took pleasure in running his hands over it as he listened to Joe's explanation.

Then Robinson lay down on deck for his afternoon nap. Above him the tip of the topmast described irregular circles. A transparent crescent moon hovered in the pure blue sky. Turning his head, Robinson saw Speranza: a strip of yellow sand, a green oval, and in the background the rugged rocky hill.

Suddenly it came to him that he would never leave the island. The *Whitebird* was a messenger from a civilization to which he had no desire to return. He felt young and strong, but he knew that if he returned to the civilized world he would soon turn into a stodgy, middle-aged man as stupid and cold-hearted as Captain Hunter and his men. His wife in York had no doubt remarried, his children were grown up and had no need of him. No, he would be faithful to the new life that Friday had taught him.

When he announced his decision to remain on the island, Joseph expressed great surprise. The captain's only reply was a cold smile. Quarters were rather cramped on the *Whitebird* and perhaps he was relieved at not having to take two passengers aboard.

"As master of the island," he said courteously, "you have been very generous with your supplies, not to mention the gold pieces my men have taken. It will give me pleasure if you accept that little gig you see on the poop deck as a reminder of our visit to Speranza. We don't need it. We have enough boats without it."

It was a light, trim craft, ideal for one or two men in good weather and a welcome replacement for Friday's old canoe. At nightfall Robinson and Friday paddled back to the island in it.

Robinson was very relieved to set foot on Speranza again. The *Whitebird* and its men had brought destruction and disorder. But what did that matter? At dawn the English vessel would weigh anchor and sail away. Robinson had given the captain to understand that he did not wish the position of his island to be made known. The captain had promised and Robinson knew he was a man of his word. Robinson and Friday still had long, happy years of solitude ahead of them.

CHAPTER SIXTEEN

The sky was barely gray
when Robinson climbed down from his araucaria. He hated
the pale dreary hours of dawn, and he seldom got up before
the first rays of the sun appeared. As for Friday, he always
slept late. That night Robinson had slept fitfully; the heavy
food he had eaten on board the *Whitebird* had given him
nightmares, and he had awakened very early.

He went down to the beach. As he had expected, the
Whitebird was gone. The water was gray and the sky color-
less. The birds were silent and the vegetation was weighed
down with heavy dew. A great sadness came over Robinson.
In a few minutes, an hour at the most, the sun would rise
and bring joy and life back to the island. In the meantime,
Robinson thought he would take a look at Friday sleeping
in his hammock. He wouldn't wake him, but Friday's mere
presence would be a comfort to him.

The hammock was empty. And still more surprising, the
baubles that Friday played with—the mirrors, flutes, blow-
pipes, darts, feathers and so on—had disappeared. Nor was

there any sign of Anda, the little goat. Robinson was filled with dread. Had Friday gone off with the *Whitebird*? He ran down to the beach. The gig and the old canoe were there, drawn up on the white sand. If Friday had gone aboard the *Whitebird*, he would have taken one of them. Why would he choose to swim in the middle of the night?

Robinson searched the island, calling out "Friday!" Stumbling and shouting, he explored the beaches, the cliffs, the dunes, the woods and the rocky hill. And little by little he gave up hope; yes, Friday must have gone off and left him. But why? Why?

Then he remembered how Friday had admired the beautiful white ship, how happy he had been climbing from spar to spar. That's what it was. Friday had been fascinated by an invention, more beautiful than all those he himself had made on the island.

Robinson recalled the gruesome stories Joseph the mate had told him about the slave trade. He felt sure that his Indian friend was already shackled and stowed away in the *Whitebird's* hold.

Overcome with grief, Robinson went on searching, but all he found were heart-breaking reminders, the aeolian harp and the kite, both smashed by the sailors. Suddenly he felt something hard under his feet. It was Tenn's collar, half rotted away. Robinson pressed his forehead against a eucalyptus trunk and wept until there were no more tears left in him.

When he raised his head, he saw five or six vultures

watching him out of their red cruel eyes. The vultures had guessed right, Robinson wanted to die, but he didn't want his body to be torn to pieces by these carrion eaters. He remembered the cave where he had spent so many happy hours.

Of course the explosion had stopped up the mouth, but there must, he thought, be some crack he could slip through. And then he would go down into his warm, comfortable hole, he would squat there with his feet crossed and his head on his knees and forget everything; he would fall asleep forever, safe from the vultures.

Slowly he made his way to the rocky hill. And indeed, after searching for some time, he found a crevice hardly big enough for a cat. But he was so shrunk with misery that he felt sure he would be able to squeeze through. He peered in to see if the passage really led into to cave. Just then he heard something moving inside. A stone fell out. Robinson jumped back. Something moved into the crevice and wriggled out of it. It was a child, holding his right arm over his forehead, perhaps to shield himself from the light, perhaps to ward off a blow. Robinson was dumbfounded.

"Who are you?" he asked. "What are you doing here?"

"I'm the cabin boy of the *Whitebird*," said the child. "I didn't like it and I've run away. Yesterday when I was waiting on the captain's table, you looked at me kindly. And then I heard you weren't going to leave. I decided to hide on the island and stay with you."

"But what about Friday? Did you see Friday?"

"Oh yes! Last night I slipped out on deck, I thought I'd try to swim ashore. And then I saw someone come alongside in a canoe. It was your servant. He had a little white goat with him. He went to the mate's cabin; the mate seemed to be expecting him. I could see he was going to stay on board. So I swam to the canoe and climbed in."

So that was why both boats were there, thought Robinson.

"And then I came here and hid," the cabin boy went on. "Now the *Whitebird* has gone without me."

"Come with me," said Robinson.

He took the cabin boy by the hand and together they climbed the rocky hill. Halfway up Robinson stopped and looked at his new friend. A faint smile lit up the thin, freckled face. Robinson released the little hand he had been holding and looked at it. It was thin and fragile, bruised by the rough work the boy had been doing on shipboard.

From the top of the hill one could see the whole island, still bathed in mist. On the beach the gig and the canoe were tossing in the rising tide. On the sea far to the north a white spot was receding toward the horizon: the *Whitebird*.

Robinson pointed toward it. "Take a good look," he said. "A ship off the coast of Speranza. That's something you may never see again."

The spot became smaller and smaller and finally disappeared. And then the sun rose. A cricket chirped. A gull glided down on the water and rose again with a little fish in its beak. One after another the flowers opened their petals.

Robinson felt life and joy returning to him. Friday had taught him how to live, and then he had gone. But Robinson was not alone. Now he had this small friend, whose hair—as red as his own—was flaming in the sun. A new life was beginning, a life as beautiful as the island that was waking in the mist at their feet.

"What is your name?" Robinson asked.

"Juan Neljapaev," said the boy. And as though to apologize for the unpronounceable name: "I was born in Estonia."

"From now on," said Robinson, "your name will be Sunday. Sunday is the day of rest, the day of laughter and games. For me you will always be Sunday's child."

ABOUT THE AUTHOR

MICHEL TOURNIER's first novel, *Friday,* won the Grand Prix du Roman of the Academie Francaise, as well as international praise and noteworthy reviews. After completing this adult book, based on the Robinson Crusoe theme, Monsieur Tournier decided to share his research and enthusiasm for the story with young readers also and so he wrote another book, *Friday and Robinson, Life on Speranza Island.*

The author's second adult novel, *Le Roi des Aulnes,* was the first book to be the unanimous winner of the Prix Goncourt, France's most prestigious literary award.

Michel Tournier lives in the Chevreuse Valley and is presently cultural consultant for a French television circuit.